What the critics are saying...

"Blood of the Raven by Anya Bast is a thrilling and erotic journey into the world of the Vampir. Grab a drink and settle in because you won't want to stop reading until the very end…" ~ *eCataromance*

5 *Stars* "Blood of the Raven is an engrossing book. It combines a mystery, a love story and hot sex so fluidly that I couldn't stop reading." ~ *Just Erotic Romance Reviews*

5 *Blue Ribbons* "I loved BLOOD OF THE RAVEN and couldn't put it down until I finished it…. This is an excellent mystery/paranormal read that will leave you looking for Anya Bast's next release." ~ *Romance Junkies*

4.5 *Stars* "Blood of the Raven is a thrilling, ass-kicking vampire romance. The atmosphere that Anya Bast portrays is intricate, dark, and highly erotic." ~ *Just Erotic Romance Reviews*

BLOOD OF THE RAVEN

ANYA BAST

Blood of the Raven
An Ellora's Cave Publication, January 2005

Ellora's Cave Publishing, Inc.
1337 Commerce Drive
Stow, Ohio 44224

ISBN #1419951483
Other available formats: ISBN MS Reader (LIT), Adobe (PDF),
Rocketbook (RB), Mobipocket (PRC) & HTML

Edited by: *Briana St. James*
Cover art by: *Syneca*

Warning:

The following material contains graphic sexual content meant for mature readers. *Blood of the Raven* has been rated *E-rotic* by a minimum of three independent reviewers.

Ellora's Cave Publishing offers three levels of Romantica™ reading entertainment: S (S-ensuous), E (E-rotic), and X (X-treme).

S-*ensuous* love scenes are explicit and leave nothing to the imagination.

E-*rotic* love scenes are explicit, leave nothing to the imagination, and are high in volume per the overall word count. In addition, some E-rated titles might contain fantasy material that some readers find objectionable, such as bondage, submission, same sex encounters, forced seductions, etc. E-rated titles are the most graphic titles we carry; it is common, for instance, for an author to use words such as "fucking", "cock", "pussy", etc., within their work of literature.

X-*treme* titles differ from E-rated titles only in plot premise and storyline execution. Unlike E-rated titles, stories designated with the letter X tend to contain controversial subject matter not for the faint of heart.

Also by Anya Bast

Blood of the Rose
Autumn Pleasures: The Union
Spring Pleasures: The Transformation
Summer Pleasures: The Capture
Winter Pleasures: The Training

BLOOD OF THE RAVEN

Anya Bast

Dedication

Dedicated to my husband, as always, for his support and love.

For Lori and Russell for their friendship.

Chapter One

"He can make you forget your own name in bed."

Fate snapped out of her reverie and blinked at her acquaintance, Cynthia Hamilton. "Excuse me?"

"That man you were just staring at." Cynthia took a sip of her white wine and glanced up to the balcony that overlooked the crowded room of charity ball-goers. A tall, broad-shouldered man with glossy black hair stood by the balustrade, watching the milling crowd below him.

Fate had noticed him earlier, since he wasn't a man easily missed. That black hair fell to the middle of his back, framing a ferociously masculine face with full, sensual lips and dark blue eyes. The shadow of a beard graced his strong, square jaw. The length of his hair didn't make him seem any less male. Fate doubted anything could weaken the powerful masculine energy the man emanated even from across a crowded room.

His tall, well-built body was clothed in an expensive-looking tux. The women did a double take when they noticed him. Interested sexual heat emanated from their designer gown-clad, workout-sculpted bodies.

Aside from his gorgeousness, Fate had noticed him earlier because he seemed familiar to her for some reason, and also simply because he was a man a woman did not glance past. But if she'd been staring at him now, she hadn't been aware of it. Too lost to other thoughts.

"That's Gabriel Letourneau," said Cynthia.

Fate nearly choked on the sip of martini she'd taken. "*That's* Gabriel Letourneau?" She knew the name well. He was the keeper of the Vampiric territory in which Newville fell, and was a member of the Council of the Embraced. Notoriously private and reclusive, it wasn't often he ventured into the public light.

"Yes." Cynthia leaned in, her dark red hair falling loose over her shoulders, and enveloped Fate in a cloud of L'Eau D'Issey. Behind them, the crowd seemed to heave and sigh. "That man fucks like he does business, ruthless, intense and all-consumed by the project...at hand." Cynthia laughed softly at her own little joke. "He's an absolute *god* in bed."

Fate eased back away from Cynthia and drained her martini. That was a bit too much information. Her companion must be a little tipsy. "Really."

"Mmmm-hmm. He's an Embraced, but I never saw any fangs during the night we spent together." She drained her glass, and then shrugged. "More's the pity."

Fate's gaze flicked back to the man. The ranks of the fully Embraced Vampir mostly kept to themselves except for the few narcissists that sought the admiration of the humans who worshipped them. For the most part the Council of the Embraced "handled" those few aberrations with their own force of peacekeepers. The attention seekers disappeared as soon as they surfaced to give a controversial interview or start their own short-lived rock band. The Embraced were feared, and therefore hated, by many activist humans. As the leaders of their kind, the keepers were the very few that were publicly known to be Vampir. They took most of the heat from those who feared the Embraced and most of the danger, too.

Fate pulled the olive off the plastic spear in her martini glass with her teeth and bit into the salty meat as she studied him. The man in question turned his head and looked at her...*right* at her. Fate straightened, her eyes widening. His gaze took her in from the top of her head to her feet, seeming to undress and caress her as it slowly slid down her body. Those sultry, full lips of his curved in a smile as he lifted his glass and took a drink.

The heated look in his blue eyes made her nipples tighten and her sex tingle—and she thought she'd been paralyzed from the neck down, a sexual quadriplegic. That man had just aroused her with one very potent look. He'd awoken her libido with a glance.

Unsettled, Fate swallowed the olive, set her glass on a nearby table and turned to look in the other direction. Instantly, she froze. Christ, what were Christopher and Lisa doing at Dorian Cross's charity ball? God, that was a dumb question. Christopher was Dorian's attorney. He *worked* for Dorian. Half of Newville did.

"He's an asshole and she's a bitch," summed up Cynthia, after her head swiveled in the direction Fate's had gone.

Fate glanced at Cynthia. "I-I have to go."

"Wait, Fate, you have to stay at least until after Mr. Cross auctions off your paintings."

Oh, God. Cynthia was right. She was trapped here for another couple of hours. Fate backed up into the crush of people behind her. Cynthia worked for Dorian Cross, too, sort of as a personal secretary. She often acted as a go-between for Fate and Dorian. "I know. I meant, I have to go—uh—powder my nose." Inwardly, she cringed. Did women ever say that in real life?

"Dorian would very much appreciate it if you stayed until the end, if possible, Fate. You're the star of this show."

Oh, God. She feigned a nod of assurance. "Of course I will."

Cynthia smiled in relief.

Fate hesitated, remembering what she'd wanted to ask, the reason she'd initiated conversation with Cynthia in the first place. "Cynthia, do you know if Dorian sent me any packages earlier today?"

Cynthia frowned. "No. I mean, if he did, he didn't tell me about it."

Fate bit her lower lip. Then who had? Granted, she was slightly relieved that the rich man who'd become the patron and benefactor of her art had perhaps not sent the gorgeous designer-made dove-gray gown and heels—not to mention the underthings, a delicate, lacey gray demi-bra, thong and silky thigh-high stockings. Nestled in the gown's box had also been a lushly packaged bottle of Sorenson's Heaven. Even poor, starving artist Fate knew that was an outrageously expensive perfume. Whoever had sent the clothing had also provided a prepaid appointment to a swanky local salon for a session of complete pampering and a makeover, of which she had availed herself.

She was glad Dorian might not be the one playing prince to her Cinderella. Fate didn't know what she'd do if he ever made that kind of an advance in her direction. But if he hadn't, then who had? Then again, maybe it had been Dorian and he hadn't wanted Cynthia to know for some reason.

Fate forced a smile. "Okay, see you later then."

"See you." Cynthia turned to greet a tall silver-haired man who'd approached her, and Fate disappeared into the crowd.

Tottering on the dove-gray four-inch heels and wishing like hell for her far less glamorous painting sweats and slippers, she made her way across the room...away from Christopher and the woman he'd left her for.

She'd celebrated New Year's Eve—nearly a year ago now—with Chris. She'd figured what better way to meet the new year than making love? Instead she'd just ended up getting fucked.

What was it with love? What made it real? Fate sure hadn't found out yet. All she'd found was self-induced illusion. It was amazing how people could delude themselves into believing someone was something they needed, when they were really just poison.

She searched the lush and glittering throng for a sign of Dorian. Crystal chandeliers glimmered above the small, intimate tables scattered about the ballroom of the Augustus hotel. The rich and fashionable elite sat at each of the small, round tables. Wide swathes of gold silk hung on the walls between her paintings and those of other local artists. Dorian had bought them all and planned to auction them off tonight for charity. Fate was Dorian's favorite artist, however, and far more of her paintings hung the walls than anyone else's.

She stopped dead in the middle of the crowd, feeling that same tingling sensation she'd had on and off for the last number of years—like she was being watched. Fate knew she had psychic ability. Once in a while, she experienced flashing visions of things that came true. Knowledge about people sometimes suddenly flooded her mind.

And the lucid dreaming.

Although, she wasn't sure if she'd use the term *lucid dreaming* for what she did. That was simply the term that came closest to defining it. Sometimes while she slept, she traveled to people's homes in the dead of night—people she would later end up meeting in waking reality. At times she'd wind up going to their homes for some reason and she'd confirm that everything she'd seen while she'd been in the dream world version of their house was correct down the exact shade of Berber covering the floor.

And other things happened while she took those trips into that other realm. Dark people stalked her, harassed her, and fought her. Were they apparitions created from the fears deep within her own subconscious mind, merely her own issues that had taken a human-like form in her psyche—her nightmares? Fate told herself they were and not something real. Not something related to the truth of the places and people she visited before she met them in waking reality.

Fate told herself they were not the Dominion, the wraiths the Embraced claimed they kept in check on the behalf of humankind. Some people believed the stories about the Dominion, those psychic vampires, and how they could wreak havoc on humankind if they had the strength and opportunity. Others thought the Embraced had simply made them up as a way to make themselves legitimate.

That she was different was a secret she kept to herself, a problem that had been barely controllable her whole life. She just wanted to fit in, but normality remained ever elusive.

She looked up toward the second floor and found Gabriel Letourneau's mesmerizing gaze locked on her. She couldn't look away.

* * * * *

Gabriel grasped the brass balcony railing and watched Fate in the crowd below him. The gown he'd sent her was perfect, as he'd known it would be—perfect for her creamy pale skin and her cool gray eyes.

He imagined the fine material stroking over her thighs like a lover's hand as she walked. He envisioned the bra that he'd selected cupping her breasts, the delicate, lacey thong pulling between her thighs with every step she took, rubbing against her clit. He wanted to lift the soft layers of her gown and slip that thong down over her hips. He could almost hear the whisper of the fabric against her skin as he slid it off.

Her long, dark brown hair was twisted up into a sleek chignon on the back of her head and secured with pearl-tipped pins. Soon, maybe tonight, he'd loose that hair so it fell down her back, allowing him to gather the weight of it in his hands. Soon, he'd have that hair spread over the mattress of his bed as he took her beneath him. She'd be soft and warm. Her breasts would fit against his palms so exquisitely. Her nipples would tighten and flush with her excitement. Her pussy would grip his cock like a tailor-made glove. Gabriel suppressed an aroused shudder and took a long drink of his bourbon.

A woman walked differently after a man had found her G-spot, a little more fluidly and with a little more roll to her hips. No man had ever found Fate's. It was Gabriel's intention to change that.

Though he knew she'd had men. Christopher Connor was one. She'd also had a couple — but just a couple — one-night stands in the months since she'd broken it off with him. Gabriel intended to be the next man she took to her bed.

It'd been close to five years since Gabriel had started watching Fate Harding. He'd been interested in her from the beginning, but after keeping such a close watch on her, enveloping her in his anonymous attention, protecting her from the dark forces at work around her, and learning all he could about her and her life, he'd become enraptured with her.

He knew her well enough to understand just how uncomfortable she was here. How badly she wanted to trade that gown for her painting sweats. Fate Harding was a bundle of contradictions. She was a sensitive, introverted and creative artist, but far from the stereotypical dreamy waif.

Her father had died when Fate was three years old. Her mother had been an alcoholic and had abused her mentally and physically. When Fate was twelve, the state discovered the abuse and took Fate away from her mother and sent her to live with her detached and uncaring aunt. She'd had a hard childhood and had been deeply hurt and betrayed by those she believed she could trust. It hadn't been easy for her, but Fate hadn't allowed her turbulent upbringing to become a chip on her shoulder. Instead, Fate had decided she would never again be a victim. As soon as she was old enough to have a part-time job, she'd saved up enough money to start taking self-defense classes. She hadn't stopped until she'd become a black belt in Tae Kwon Do.

Gabriel knew she'd done it to make sure she could always take care of herself, since she knew there was no one else to do it. He'd spent the last couple centuries amassing a fortune for the same underlying reason, so he understood the motivation well. The need to feel some sense of control over your own destiny. A sense of safety.

Yes, he understood her well because in some ways they were very similar.

Now that his period of watching had come to a close, it was time she learned who he was. It was time he became visible to her.

If only for one night. Then he could say goodbye.

He wanted to feel the soft slide of her body over his, her hair brushing his chest as he rolled her beneath him on the bed. He wanted make her scream in passion and claw the sheets, come so hard she brought him with her.

Below him, Fate stilled in the middle of the crowd and looked up. He held her gaze with his until she could have no doubt about his interest in her. Then a drunken guest bumped into her, nearly spilling his drink down the front of her gown, and the spell was broken. Fate glanced up at him once more, then turned and disappeared into the crowd.

Gabriel set his drink down on a table and descended the stairs, lightly willing the humans out of his way with a small bit of glamour. After picking up two flutes of champagne, he found Fate in the crowd. He followed behind her, keeping his eyes on the sensual swish of her skirts as she walked.

Christopher Connor intercepted her before Gabriel could. When Connor approached, Gabriel felt the shocked unease within Fate through the one-way mental link

Gabriel had forged with her. She didn't want to talk to this man who'd injured her so deeply, and had betrayed her trust and love, like so many others.

Gabriel hung back, and pitched his hearing to listen and watch from afar, as he'd listened and watched her for the last five years.

"You move fast, Fate. I've been trying to catch up with you," said Connor.

Fate stiffened visibly. "Why?"

Connor smiled slowly, revealing the dimples Gabriel was certain that women loved—though he knew they didn't work on Fate anymore. "I wanted to offer my congratulations. Your art has really grown wings."

"Big of you to say, Chris. You never thought my paintings were any good."

"That's not true. I just thought—"

"I should commercialize more." Gabriel could scent the hot anger that flashed through her even at a distance, even through the crowd.

He shrugged and a look of exasperation crossed his handsome face. "You have to go where the money is." He paused, looking her up and down. "You look absolutely stunning this evening." Gabriel could hear the note of desire in Connor's voice. Gabriel's hands clenched on the stems of the champagne flutes.

Fate sighed. "Where's your date?"

"Lisa? She's around." He smiled again. "Does it matter? Fate, she and I, we're not as good as you and I were."

Fate went silent for a moment. Gabriel felt emotions swirling within her, not the least of which was deep resentment. "You and I were never good, Chris."

Connor leaned toward her and lowered his voice. "I don't know about that. I can remember one place where we were pretty good together."

"Maybe from your perspective. I never thought it was much good." Fate took a step back and Gabriel moved fast, ensuring she backed up against him. Holding the champagne flutes in one hand, he placed his other hand on her waist and pressed his chest to her back. She looked up at him and let out a surprised gasp but didn't move away.

"Are you all right, *ma cheri*?" Gabriel asked. "I go to get drinks and come back to find you talking to—" Gabriel flicked an irritated glance at Connor "—what's your name?"

"Christopher Connor. I'm Fate's former *fiancé*."

"Fiancé?" he raised an eyebrow and exaggerated his almost completely faded French accent on purpose. Gabriel leaned down, inhaling the scent of Fate's skin, and brushed his lips against her cheek. It was absolute heaven to finally touch her after so long only dreaming about it. Fate didn't move away; instead she snuggled back against him and let out a contented sigh. "Should I be jealous, *ma cheri*?" Gabriel growled into her ear just loud enough for Connor to hear.

Fate hesitated a moment, closing her eyes at his touch. Gabriel's confidence grew. Then she straightened and looked pointedly at Connor. "No, you have no reason to be jealous at all...*darling*." She cocked her head. "Christopher was just leaving."

Connor went silent, narrowing his eyes at her. He tipped his head toward Gabriel. "Have a nice evening." He backed away into the crowd.

"God, what an asshole," Fate muttered under her breath. She turned to him. "Thank you so much, Mr...?"

Gabriel pressed a flute of champagne into her hand. "Gabriel Letourneau."

"I-I actually knew that. You're the keeper of Embraced here in Newville."

"I am. I hope you do not hold the same prejudices and fears so many others seem to have about us." He knew she didn't. Fate had even participated in a rally once when an ultraconservative senator in Mississippi had tried to push a bill through Congress that would've declared open season on the Demi and the Vampir. As if the humans could locate and kill all the Embraced. As if the humans could survive the Dominion on their own if they ever succeeded. It was a ridiculous notion. They didn't understand the checks and balances in place to ensure the survival of their race. They didn't understand the payoffs and sacrifices they needed to make to maintain it.

She shook her head. "Not at all." She held out her hand. "My name is Fate. Fate Harding."

He took her hand and, instead of shaking it, brought it to his mouth. He flipped it and laid a careful, deliberate kiss to the pulse at her wrist, flicking his tongue out minutely to taste her skin. Her heart rate sped up under his lips. Gabriel suppressed a groan. She tasted so sweet. Her blood would be like sipping heaven. Reluctantly, he released her hand. "And *I* knew that."

She raised an eyebrow. "You did?"

He indicated a wall behind him where some of her lush, nearly erotic, artwork hung. Fate used dark, muted colors and her subjects were generally locked in heated embraces, on the brink of a kiss, or teasingly and temptingly on the verge of some other activity. They were generally provocative works, seething with dark angst. They revealed a concealed passion within the artist. Gabriel wanted to unlock that passion he knew Fate masked. She just needed the right man with the right key. He felt sure he had it. "You're the artist."

She lowered her eyes, her lashes shadowing her cheeks, and took a drink of her champagne. "Yes."

"Your work is highly sensual, Fate. I enjoy it very much. I bought several pieces from the Eastside Gallery last year. I intend to purchase more this evening."

She looked up at him in silence for a heartbeat, her full red lips parted in wonder. As though she couldn't believe people actually enjoyed her paintings. "Thank you."

Gabriel glanced to the left where Connor stood, watching them. Fate's gaze followed the direction of his narrowed eyes.

Gabriel couldn't help himself, even though he knew it might scare her off. He took a step toward her, closing the small distance between them. "Maybe you should kiss me. You know, to complete the illusion."

She smiled and tipped her head to side coyly. "Kiss you?"

Gabriel smiled back. He held her gaze for a long heartbeat, feeling their shared connection born of strong and good chemistry. Gabriel knew Fate felt it every bit as much as he did. "Only for show, you understand."

She stepped forward and tipped her face to his. He twined an arm around her waist and pressed her to him. The activity around them ceased to be of any importance. It ceased to *exist*. He lowered his head and let his lips hover over hers, inhaling the heady scent of her breath and noting how it came faster, before he brushed his lips over hers.

He'd imagined kissing her...and doing so much more to her for so long. She tasted every bit as sweet as he'd fantasized she would.

Rubbing his thumb back and forth over the exposed skin at the small of her back, he crushed his mouth to hers. Her lips relented beneath his and parted. He swept his tongue into heaven. A multitude of fantasies rode him hard, made him want to pick her up, carry her to some secluded area of the hotel and act every one of them out.

He worked his mouth over hers, tasting, possessing. Her breasts pressed up against his chest and her hips brushed against him. He wanted to strip her clothes off now and lay her down on the floor. He wanted to savor the cream of her sex on his tongue, slip his cock into her and drive them both to climax.

But something irritating scrabbled at the outer edges of his awareness. Someone tapped a microphone. The crowd hushed. "I want to welcome everyone to this year's charity ball and auction..."

Dorian Cross's voice droned on about something far less important than Gabriel's mouth on Fate's.

"...overriding number of the paintings are Fate Harding's. So without further delay, I'd like to ask the star of this auction up here to say a few words. Fate?"

Fate pushed against his chest and pulled away, and he let her...reluctantly. She looked up at him with heavy eyelids and a languorous look on her face. She raised an eyebrow. "Really too bad that was only for show and not a promise of something *more* tonight."

Gabriel smiled. She was *perfect*. "Well—"

"Fate?" Dorian called again from the podium. "Fate, are you here?"

"Damn. I have to go." She backed away, set her champagne flute on a nearby table and hurried through the crowd toward the podium.

Gabriel covertly adjusted his rigid cock in his pants and watched her take the microphone.

"She's sweet little piece of ass."

Gabriel turned to see Adam Ridge standing beside him. The Vampir aided him in the management of Newville's population of Embraced, though Gabriel intended to soon divest him of that position of power. Adam was rash—a loose cannon. He'd flaunted the laws of their kind too many times. He was young by Embraced standards, only about 160 years old, and he was an American of the worst kind, straight from the Wild West. He planned on having a long discussion with Adam tomorrow. It was past time he did it.

"What are you doing here?" Gabriel asked in a tight voice.

Adam gave a slow smile. "I crashed."

"She's an *unmarked* sweet little piece of ass."

Gabriel turned at the familiar voice that still held a trace of cultured Bostonian accent after all these years, to find Charles Scythchilde on his other side. Charlie was even younger than Adam, but far more mature and responsible. Charlie had been at Gabriel's side for a very long time, since the late 1800s in New York City, Gabriel's former territory. "What is this, a reunion of the Embraced? Is Niccolo here, too?"

"*I* had an invitation," commented Charlie, casting a look of scorn in Adam's direction. "Niccolo did not attend. Though he, too, had an invitation."

"Niccolo isn't much for parties," said Gabriel.

"Niccolo isn't much for anything these days," remarked Charlie.

It was true. Niccolo was one of Gabriel's most trusted friends, and far, *far* older than any of them. Niccolo was taciturn and stoic at the best of times, but lately he'd grown even more remote.

"So, what's with you and the fascination with that woman, Gabe?" asked Adam. He took a sip of what looked to be whiskey as he eyed Fate making her remarks on the podium. "I mean she's pretty and all but she's an unmarked human."

"That's why he likes them, Adam," replied Charlie. "He can fuck them and leave them. Easy. Uncomplicated. It's not like they share our world. Gabriel doesn't want to get heavily involved with a woman, be they human, Vampir, or Demi."

Gabriel took a drink of champagne, his gaze fixed on Fate. "Thanks for that little bit of psychoanalysis, Charlie. It's good you never decided to take it up as a profession." Although he mostly fed from the Demi-Vampir, the vampiric class that lived from sex, not blood, it was true that he'd been with many human women. To a human, the bite of a Vampir was beyond orgasmic. It could cause a human to become addicted if they sought the experience too often. That was why he nearly never bit. If he did, he used glamour to cause the woman to forget the experience and he healed up the wound.

And he *never* spent more than one night in a woman's bed.

"Is she tonight's conquest, Gabe?" asked Adam. "A little late-night snack?"

At the front of the room, Dorian Cross had taken the microphone back and was introducing the man who would conduct the auction. On the left side of the room, hotel employees were handing out auction paddles.

Gabriel smiled. "She's far more than just a late-night snack, Adam," he answered finally. He flicked him a cold glance. "But, unlike you, Adam, I do not flaunt the rules that the Council of the Embraced have set down. I will not bite her. For breaking those rules, you may find yourself knocked down several notches in this territory very soon."

Adam paled. Good. He understood the threat behind those words.

"She's the one you've been watching, isn't she? The human dreamwalker," said Charlie.

"Yes, and she's a very powerful one." Without waiting for a reply, Gabriel walked away to get a good seat for the auction.

* * * * *

Fate pulled on her coat and scanned the crowd one last time. Gabriel Letourneau had bought every one of her paintings.

Every. Single. One.

There was something approaching erotic in the idea that her paintings—a little bit of her own soul—would be hanging in that man's home. Her thoughts, ideas, and desires had gone into every single stroke of the brush on the canvas. It was a subconscious imprint of herself, an intimate part of her psyche.

She wanted to thank him for his generosity. And, *damn*, she wanted to kiss him again. It had been incredible, spine-tingling, and toe-curling. She'd never been kissed like that. Never in her life. No…it hadn't even been a kiss. It had been Gabriel making love to her mouth. His lips had seduced hers at first, sliding over them in a light tasting. Then he'd slanted his mouth over hers and taken her in a deep, penetrating kiss that had shot lust straight down to her pussy.

Fate hadn't felt that level of desire in years. Maybe never.

And his voice and accent. Fate drew a breath. Nearly all the French had been bled from his deep, velvety voice, but there was still enough to make her spine tingle. She'd like to have him for a night, just for one night, in her bed.

After he'd kissed her, she'd still been shaking when she reached the podium. She'd been flushed the whole way through her remarks.

Now it seemed Gabriel had left. Maybe he made an ordinary practice of stalking women down with that predatory, sexual light in his eyes, kissing the hell out of them, casually dropping twenty grand for charity and then disappearing.

Man, it had been a strange night. A strange day.

She wondered if it had been Gabriel who sent her the package. Could it be? Mentally, she shook her head. No way. Despite his apparent interest in her and despite the fact he seemed vaguely familiar, they'd never met before tonight. She would definitely remember if she had. Gabriel wasn't the kind of man you forgot.

With one last look around the ballroom, she buttoned her long black coat and headed out to the lobby. She squinted at the glass doors leading out onto the street and frowned. It was raining. Hard. Her heels clicked on the marble floor of the entranceway of the hotel. She nodded and smiled at guests who were slowly filtering out of the ball.

A couple walked in front of her, also on their way out. The female portion of the couple squealed as she walked out into the rain. The man, apparently her husband or boyfriend, opened his umbrella and ushered her beneath it. He wrapped an arm around her waist to keep her out of the downpour and laid a kiss to her temple.

Something in Fate's stomach twisted at the sight.

The day she'd caught Christopher cheating on her, she'd taken paint to canvas like a mourner to the veil. She'd painted into the early morning, her tears blurring her vision and obscuring the work on the canvas. She'd really loved the bastard. Well, she'd loved the illusion of him. The illusion of what she'd thought their life together would be. The reality had been somewhat different.

Fate stepped out the brass and glass front doors of the hotel and approached the group of bustling valets. She hadn't felt comfortable handing the keys to her dented seven-year-old Honda Accord over to the valet while they were parking shiny new Towncars and Cadillacs, but she'd done it anyway. Walking down a deserted city street at one in the morning wasn't her idea of a good time, black belt in Tai Kwon Do or not. All the fighting she'd ever done was in the competition ring or the *dojang*—never on the street, and never against anyone who actually meant to harm her outside competition.

With Dorian's generous patronage, she would now be able to afford a new car. She wasn't sure why she had the vague feeling she was selling her soul to the devil for it, though. Dorian had not asked anything of her she didn't want to give, had never asked her to compromise herself or her art.

Not yet, anyway.

Fate maintained her right to suspect his intentions.

One of the valets approached her and she gave him her ticket. "Be right back, miss," he said, and then hurried away.

The cold December wind whipped around the buildings, down the streets and slapped the breath out of her as she stood waiting by the doors, safely out of the cold November rain.

The valet pulled her car around and she hurried as quickly as she could on teetery high heels over wet pavement—which wasn't very quickly at all—down the steps. The valet met her with his umbrella and ushered her the rest of the way into her vehicle. Before getting into the car, she pressed a hefty tip into his palm. She wanted to share her good fortune. Despite the umbrella-laden valet, she was soaked by the time she sat down in the driver's seat and slammed the door closed.

"Yuck!" she said. Her hair had come down in sodden clumps around her face and quick glance in the rearview mirror confirmed her suspicion about her mascara. Well, it wasn't like she was going anywhere but home, anyway. Her lovely vampiric quarry had escaped her, after all. Tonight, only one would occupy her bed.

How depressing.

She threw her purse onto the passenger's seat, flicked her windshield wipers on and pulled out into the street. There were very few residential areas in downtown Newville, mostly just office buildings and closed-up shops. At one in the morning, everything was absolutely still and quiet.

She turned a corner and flipped on her CD player so that Seether could sing about love-stained hands. Strangely, something niggled way down deep within. Her sixth sense, if that's what it was, kicked it up a notch along with a feeling of being watched. Which was silly. She was *moving*, after all, and there was no one behind her, or in front of her—or anywhere at all around her, for that matter. There was no one around to observe her.

But, still.

This was a far different feeling from the mere tingling she'd had before. This felt antagonistic, not simply watchful and interested. This was a heavy, dark feeling— the feeling of someone wishing to harm her. And she would take it seriously. After all, it wasn't as if she lived in a world of mere mortals. Other, far more powerful, creatures lurked in the shadowy city.

"Fine," she muttered as she surrendered to her intuition. She stopped at a red light. It was probably nothing more than her runaway imagination. Still, she groped for the handle of her glove compartment and opened it. Her Smith & Wesson lay comfortably within. It wouldn't hurt to have it near.

At the same time her hand closed around her gun the dark feeling of foreboding deepened in pitch, hummed for a heartbeat and then exploded in her head.

They were coming for her. She knew it for certain in that one moment.

Everything happened too quickly for her to register each individual event. Two dark figures rushed her car— one on the passenger side, the other on the driver's side.

She straightened, her gun in hand, and slammed on the gas. Her car moved about a foot before the engine sputtered and died. She coasted to the middle of the intersection.

What the hell?

The figures still advanced.

Adrenaline rushed through her, screaming for fight or flight. She chose *fight*. Since she had a clear shot at the one rushing her passenger side, she raised her gun, sighted a line of fire and pulled the trigger. The passenger side window shattered and the loud sound of the gun firing in her car nearly exploded her eardrums. Everything went eerily silent for a moment and the chokingly strong scent of sulfur filled the air.

The man kept coming.

She raised the gun and shot again. This time she hit his shoulder. He lurched to the side, shouting out obscenities and holding his arm, but he still kept on coming. Who was this guy, Superman? She trained her gun on the figure, this time aiming for his stomach. In the same moment, the driver's side window smashed.

Hard hands grabbed her shoulders. She struggled and shifted her aim to point-blank range on her attacker. Right as she pulled the trigger, he pushed her arm and her shot went wide, blowing a hole in her windshield.

With unimaginable strength, her attacker pulled her through the car window. She cried out as the broken auto glass ripped through her clothing and into her flesh when she was dragged over the shards. The man dealt with her easily, as though she weighed nothing. That's when she realized that whatever he was, it wasn't human. They struggled for a moment as she tried to turn far enough to shoot, and she drew blood from his forearm with her nails. He grasped her wrist and squeezed...really hard. She gasped in pain and dropped her gun. The man kicked it and it went skittering across the pavement.

Every bit of hope she had plummeted straight to her toes.

Both figures were hooded and dressed in black. The man who held her in this iron grasp had to be Vampir. Were both of them?

She stood in the middle of the street, her back pressed against the Vampir's. Her breath came fast and heavy and showed in the cold air. The rain still fell. The other man — the one who'd come up on her passenger side — approached her. She watched him carefully, her mind clicking over possibilities for escape.

Her car's engine turned over, startling her, and the radio turned on. The CDs in the changer in her trunk flipped one-by-one, as though someone was selecting one. Finally, the fourth CD — Nine Inch Nails — began playing.

The other had come to stand in front of her. "Better," he commented from the depths of his hood. The material of his long coat, where it covered the shoulder she'd shot, was wet with his blood, she noted with no small measure of satisfaction. He stepped toward her. Using the man holding her from behind as leverage she kicked up high and hard, nailing the man in the eye with her very sharp heel. He screamed and collapsed to the ground, holding the hand of his uninjured arm to his face.

He seemed more vulnerable by the moment. It looked like at least one of them was not a Vampir. The one she kicked could be a human under the influence of vampiric glamour. That would account for the fact that the bullet in his shoulder had barely slowed him down.

To loosen the bear hug of the man who held her, she dropped low and thrust her elbows up, twisting out of his grasp at the same time. She turned, brought the flat of her palm up hard toward his face, intending to smash his nose.

If he'd been human, it probably would have worked.

With mind-numbing speed, he grabbed her wrist and twisted it behind her back. Then he slammed her bone-jarringly hard to the street, knocking the breath out of her. Her cheek hit the pavement and she stared straight ahead at the tire of her car—at the raindrops splashing onto the road. It was as if she could see them hit one-by-one. Plink by relentless plink, they pooled like small lakes of teardrops on the pavement. The loud angry music coming from her car was all she could hear.

The Vampir grabbed her hair and jerked her head to the side, exposing her neck. Terror bubbled up within Fate as the dark, hooded head dipped to hers like some macabre lover ready to bestow a kiss. Fangs ripped into the tender flesh of her throat.

Fate regained her breath and screamed.

Chapter Two

It had taken Gabriel much longer to purchase the paintings and arrange to have them delivered to his house than he'd wanted. It hadn't helped that a local businessman he was acquainted with had waylaid him and engaged him in conversation. All the time his acquaintance was telling him how successful the ball must have been for Dorian Cross, and pitching an "interesting new investment", Gabriel had only been able to think about Fate. He could still smell her, still feel the way her lips had parted under his, how her breasts had felt against his chest.

God, his cock ached to slide into her. She'd be so tight, so soft, and so hot. He hadn't felt this much desire for a woman since…well, since he'd been human. That had been a long time ago.

Perhaps it was because he'd watched her for so long. Watched her without the ability to touch her, or to take her. Gabriel was not used to being denied the things he wanted and he'd desired Fate from the very first time he'd seen her. Now he could finally have her and his plans were being thwarted.

He scanned the ballroom. Most of the guests had left and it seemed as though Fate had gone with them. He cursed under his breath in three languages.

He'd wanted to invite her out for one more drink and use the opportunity to seduce an invitation back to her apartment. Now he'd have to find another way to get close to her. Some other pretense to draw her out.

While he walked toward the hotel lobby, he turned various possibilities over in his mind. Wondering if she was at home yet, Gabriel opened the mental connection.

And encountered deep silence. *Absolute nothingness.*

His steps faltered, and then sped up. There should not be stillness. Even when Fate slept, there was warmth, activity. Not even death brought this level of profound silence. Either the link was broken or something with Fate was very, very wrong.

Gabriel had lived long enough to know that the latter was probably true.

Gabriel pushed through the hotel's front doors. He noted briefly that it must've rained. The pavement was wet. He grabbed the first valet he saw. "Did you bring a car around for a woman with upswept brown hair and gray eyes? She was wearing a long black coat. You'd remember her car; it's an old beat-up Honda Accord." He'd been in the United States so long his accent had faded, but his agitation made it strong once more.

The valet looked at him with a blank expression on his face.

Gabriel fought the urge to shake him. "*Merde!* Answer me!"

"I remember her. I held an umbrella for her. She gave me a nice tip," said another of the attendants behind him.

Gabriel released the mute one and turned. "Do you remember if she took a right or a left onto the street?" There were two different ways Fate could've taken home.

"She went that way." The man pointed down the dark street, to the right. "That was a while ago, though. You probably won't catch her."

"There's a hundred dollars in it for you if you can bring my car around in under two minutes," said Gabriel.

The attendant moved as though his life depended on it and earned his hundred.

Gabriel slipped behind the wheel of his SUV and drove down the block. His keen vision searched the street for any sign of Fate as he traveled to her apartment.

Then his headlights flashed on her car.

It stood in the middle of an intersection. Both windows on the driver and passenger sides were smashed and there was a bullet hole through the windshield. Gabriel stopped behind the vehicle and got out. The smell of fresh blood painted the air, mixing with the remnants of human fear. His own fear tightened hard and fast within him. He forced himself to remain calm, to stay collected, so he could read any clues and discover what had happened.

His shoes crunched on glass as he approached the driver's side. Fate's purse lay on the passenger seat.

Kneeling, he examined the pavement. Drops of blood scattered the ground. He touched each one and brought it to his nose, finding the blood of a human male. He moved closer to the car and found more blood. Fear ripped through him as he determined that some of the blood droplets were from a human female.

And some were of a Vampir.

Gabriel let loose a string of curses.

Niccolo. He mentally trolled for his executioner and his territory's liaison to the human police department.

Yes, Niccolo answered after a moment.

I think we might have a rogue Vampir on our hands. Are there any in the city you haven't taken down?

I took one last night, Gabriel. Other than him, there are no rogues I'm aware of right now.

Great. A new one. I'm at the scene of what appears to be a carjacking and abduction at the corner of Chestnut and Fifth, but I know a Vampir is behind it. There's the blood of a fully Embraced here. I can't tell the sex, but I'm betting male. There's the blood of a human male, as well — likely under the influence of some heavy glamour. Gabriel sighed. *They targeted Fate Harding.* Niccolo knew that Gabriel had been keeping her under close surveillance.

The one you've been protecting?

Ironic, isn't it? Tonight had been the first night in five years he'd finally convinced himself Fate wasn't in danger and never had been.

I'm there. Will you call Samantha? asked Niccolo.

I'll tell her to bring the squad and you'll meet them here.

Fate Harding. That seems a strange coincidence, Gabriel. Niccolo severed the mental connection.

Since the unmasking of the Embraced to the humans during the battle against the Dominion in 1890, there had been much tumult in the U.S. as the government decided "what to do with them". One large problem had been the fact that the police really couldn't do much against out-of-control Vampir. So they'd established federal and local divisions for the investigation of Embraced activity in order to see to that particular policing need. They were called SPAVA, Squad for Paranormal and Vampiric Activity.

SPAVA's primary weapons against the Embraced were batons with retractable hawthorn tips, since the only surefire way for a human to kill an Embraced was stabbing one with that particular type of wood. The chemical changes that occurred when a person was Embraced made him or her highly allergic to hawthorn. If stabbed anywhere on the body, it would poison the blood of the Embraced, though the poison wouldn't be what killed the victim. The wound created by a hawthorn stake wouldn't close up, and usually the inflicted Embraced would die of blood loss, ironically enough.

Despite SPAVA, the bulk of the policing of the Embraced was still done by their own peacekeeping force of executioners. In fact, the Embraced weren't doing anything they hadn't already been doing since the dawn of civilization. They still used their force of executioners to rein in and control those that went rogue or broke the laws set forth by the Council of the Embraced. The humans had just complicated the process with paperwork and oversight committees. It made humankind feel safer and more in control.

Niccolo had been an executioner, hunting down rogue Vampir for centuries before Gabriel had been born. He'd been the natural choice to head up the division in Gabriel's territory.

Forcing himself to remain calm, Gabriel reached into the car and pulled Fate's cell phone from her purse, called the police department, and asked to speak to Detective Ripley.

"Gabriel? This is Ripley," came Samantha's smooth voice. "What's wrong?"

"We have a rogue on our hands. Get your squad to Chestnut and Fifth. Niccolo will meet you there and explain."

"Fucking Vampir," she cursed. "Can't you keep your people under control, Gabriel?"

"I don't have time to chat, Samantha. Niccolo, who is one Vampir I *know* you won't cuss at, will be able indulge you." He snapped the phone closed.

Gabriel surveyed the scene with rising rage. He'd known other humans who'd been hurt and killed by the Vampir, but this was different. *This* made him realize how deeply he cared about Fate.

Niccolo wouldn't take care of this one. Gabriel would do it personally.

He needed to change his clothes. He needed weapons. Then he'd go hunting with Niccolo when Niccolo was finished dealing with the humans.

Gabriel got into his car and sped home. The trip was a blur of the huge homes of old Newville, and then the area referred to as the Highlands. Finally Gabriel pulled into St. Anne Court and his driveway. It was a large, historic home. Somehow, Gabriel felt more comfortable there because it was from a bygone age, like himself.

A bundle swathed in black lay heaped in front of his door. Gabriel approached it carefully. As he came closer, he noted a long tendril of glossy brown hair spread on his porch. He frowned. It was the same shade as…

"Fate!" Gabriel knelt and gathered her up in his arms. She moaned.

"Fate, are you all right?" He smoothed the hair away from her face and tipped her head to the side. Deep puncture wounds marred the smooth skin of her throat.

They were painful-looking, and obviously they'd been made in rage. Blood had dripped from the wound down the plump of her breasts and onto her gown. A bruise was also blooming on her cheekbone and her lip was split. There was no telling what other injuries she'd sustained.

"Gabriel?" she rasped. Her eyes showed deep confusion. "I feel strange. Why am I here? What happened?"

She vibrated differently now. Not like a human. The bastard had Embraced her. That's why he hadn't felt her through the mental link. As soon as she'd passed out of the realm of being human, it had closed. The attacker had Embraced her and left her on his doorstep.

Why?

"The person who did this to you made you drink blood, didn't they, Fate?" he asked.

She gripped the lapels of his coat and stared up at him. Her breath hit the cold air and showed white. She nodded. Her eyes were dark, shadowed. "Lots of blood," she whispered.

"Hell." He scooped her into his arms and stood. Using telekinesis, he opened his front door. It slammed into the wall in his rage and shook the long stained glass panels embedded in it.

His home was decorated comfortably with large overstuffed furniture in dark greens, natural wood floors, and various pieces of artwork he'd picked up over the years that had pleased him. Every bit of it seemed to tremble under the energy field of his fury.

He climbed the stairs and entered his bedroom on the second floor. As soon as he laid Fate down on his four-poster bed, he began divesting her of her clothing to make sure she had no more wounds. He slipped off her long black coat and threw it to the floor angrily.

Her gown was ripped at the seams, exposing lots of creamy white skin. One side was split all the way up to under her arm, revealing the thong he'd bought her. This was not the way he'd wanted to first see her wearing it.

His hands stilled. Incredible sexual arousal was a natural side effect of the Embrace. She was not acting aroused now, which meant she must've gone through that phase either alone on his porch...or with the attacker.

"Did anyone rape you, Fate?" His voice sounded low, dangerous to his own ears. It would be more likely she would've raped the attacker. Still, if she'd been touched...

She shook her head and began to shiver violently. "Not...sexually." Her teeth chattered. The shivering was also a part of the process of the Embrace. The chemicals in the blood she drank from her attacker were changing her body at the DNA level and the process was not gentle. Especially since she was not marked. She'd never been meant to go through this process.

The Embrace did not kill a person and resurrect their body, like the vampire lore asserted. The Vampir and Demi were not the walking dead. But the Embrace did completely change a person's biological makeup. Essentially, it transformed them into a different race.

Quickly, Gabriel pulled her shoes, gown and stockings off, leaving her clad in only her bra and thong. Even now, even in this situation, his body responded to hers. He couldn't help but note her full, lush breasts spilling over the top of her demi-bra and the way the thong fit so perfect and snug over her sex. He couldn't seem to drink his fill of the sight of her, but now was hardly the time. He finished examining her and found some bruises, a few blood-clotted gashes likely made from being pulled through the shattered car window, but nothing broken or life-threatening. Nothing that the process of the Embrace would not heal.

Gabriel drew the down comforter back and lifted Fate under it. Then he crawled into the bed beside her and pulled her to his chest. Gently, he released all the pins from her hair, letting what hadn't already come loose fall long and thick around her shoulders.

There was nothing he could do for her now. The next phase of the Embrace of an unmarked human was unconsciousness. She would awaken either fully Embraced or a Demi-Vampir.

A Demi. That's probably how the attacker thought she'd end up. Most unmarked humans were not strong enough to pass through the Demi phase of the Embrace and become a fully Embraced Vampir. It would doom her to an immortal life of feeding from sex. From the lusts of others. They were literally a tier lower on the food chain. The Vampir fed from the Demi, who in turn fed mostly from the humans. Such had always been the way of it.

Gabriel could see no other reason for the viciousness of Embracing an unmarked human who did not wish to become one of them. As it appeared right now, the attacker wanted to punish Gabriel and Fate for some unknown reason. The attacker wanted to force Gabriel to watch Fate become Demi. And the bastard may have succeeded.

But for what purpose?

Gabriel held her tight and stroked her hair. Her eyelids drooped. "Fight through, Fate." It seemed like such a silly thing to say. She wouldn't be able to do anything except hang on and go for the ride.

"Gabriel," she murmured. Then her eyes closed.

He laid her back against the pillows. A silky tendril of her hair slipped through his fingers to rest on his palm. He studied it for a moment, and then fisted it in his hand. Maybe she'd been Embraced because of him. Maybe someone was using her to rile him. If it was true, it was working. And, if it was true, they'd pay dearly.

And he knew where the list of suspects began.

* * * * *

Gabriel slammed the door open to Raven House, the communal home of the Embraced. It sat near downtown, not far from his home. At one time all the keepers, including himself, had kept houses of "ill repute". Throughout history they'd served as a place where the Demi could live and work as prostitutes, providing them with an easy way to find humans to feed from. Times had changed, however, and with them social conventions and attitudes toward sex. It was now far easier for the Demi to find sources of food. All the Demi had to do was pick a willing man or woman up in a bar these days. Gabriel had kept the idea of the house, however. It served as a base of operations and a place where the Vampir and Demi could live, if they chose.

Tonight, he was looking for one resident and one resident only.

Ignoring the greetings of the Demi and Vampir who socialized in the large living room, his gaze swept the lower level, taking in the plush burgundy furnishings and those who reclined on them, and scanned the faces of those who sat at the long dining room table. Not seeing the one he hunted among them, Gabriel sought the stairs and ascended them.

He found him in the corridor. "Tell me you didn't do it, Adam," he growled as he stalked toward him. Adam had just gotten out of the shower, apparently. His hair was wet and he had a towel wrapped around his midsection.

Adam ran a hand through his short blond hair. "Gabe? What's got your panties in a bun—"

Gabriel threw him against the wall and held him there. Adam's feet dangled an inch above the floor. "Tell me you didn't do it," he repeated.

"Shit, Gabe, I don't know what the hell you're talking about."

"Where were you after the charity ball tonight? Where'd you go?"

Adam paled.

Gabriel shook him when he failed to answer. "You better come up with something good, Adam. Something I can verify. Where did you go after the ball ended and what did you do?"

Adam hesitated before speaking. "I-I'm sorry, Gabe. It was wrong. I know it was. I couldn't help myself."

Bloody hell.

Gabriel hissed through his teeth, his jaw clenched. "Did you think I wouldn't know who did it?" He roared in anguish and released Adam. "*Mon dieu!* How could you do that, Adam? How could you put me in this position? I trusted you. *Tu m'as vraiment decu.* You truly deceived me."

Gabriel grabbed Adam's throat. Adam's brown eyes widened and he grasped Gabriel's wrists with an iron-strong grip. Two Vampir going head-to-head was never pretty.

"Hold!" roared Niccolo from the top of the stairs. "Gabriel, release him."

"We all know his proclivities, Niccolo. Adam Embraced Fate, an unmarked human, to get back at me for divesting him of his responsibilities in this territory."

Adam's eyes widened. He tried to speak and Gabriel squeezed his throat until he made a garbled choking sound.

"I heard the exchange. Get a hold of your emotions and *let him go!*" Niccolo stalked toward them. "What possible reason would Adam have for doing such a thing? Control your rage and think for a moment, Gabriel!"

Gabriel didn't move.

"Don't make me get mad," Niccolo said in a low voice. "You won't like it."

Gabriel clenched his jaw and stared at Adam. Tense silence filled the hallway and Gabriel could hear a few Demi at the top of the stairs, the ones curious enough, or stupid enough, to brave his wrath.

Gabriel released Adam. "Fine."

Adam collapsed to the floor, gasping for air and coughing. It was hard to kill a Vampir, but not impossible—easier for one Vampir to kill another.

"I didn't—" Adam gasped then fell into a coughing fit. "I didn't *Embrace* anyone," he finally choked out.

"Tell him what you did do, Adam," said Niccolo. His dark brown eyes stayed on Gabriel's face.

Adam sat up, rested his back against the wall of the hallway and rescued the towel from sliding down his waist. Then he looked up at Gabriel with a smirk and that same insolent Adamish glint in his eye. "I seduced a human woman at the ball and fed from her. I didn't use glamour on her afterward so I could have the pleasure of her remembering her gratification. And she *was* very gratified." Adam's grin widened. "Three times."

That was Adam's forte.

He broke the rules Gabriel set up all the time. Gabriel set them up and Adam knocked them down. It was too dangerous these days for the Embraced to take blood from humans without using glamour to mask the memory. Too many people wanted to crush the Vampir. Too many groups were just waiting for an excuse to take away their rights and freedoms. It was the reason Gabriel was rescinding Adam's position in management of the territory.

But all that seemed so minor now, compared to the attack against Fate.

"I suspected as much," said Niccolo.

"I'm sure she will gladly give me an alibi," continued Adam. He smirked. "She wants to see me again."

Gabriel stared down at Adam. He was a loose cannon—a wild and free man from a time and place where *wild* and *free* was the order of the day. Was it truly surprising Adam had trouble with self-control? Gabriel studied him, a muscle working in his jaw.

"Do you really think Adam is vicious enough to Embrace an unmarked human?" asked Niccolo. "Adam is trouble half the time, yes, but he's not violent."

Niccolo's words sunk past the rage and pain that had consumed—the emotions that had compelled him to Raven House in the first place. Gabriel knew he'd been consumed with strong feelings that had had no outlet. "Maybe — maybe I overreacted," he said, finally.

"You overreacted, yes," answered Niccolo. "The strong emotion you feel as a result of Fate's attack blinded you, turned friends into enemies."

Gabriel drew a deep breath. "You may be right." He leaned down and offered his hand to Adam. Adam took it warily and Gabriel pulled him up. "I'm sorry I acted so rashly."

"I'm just glad Niccolo came along before you killed me."

"You must get your emotions under control, Gabriel," said Niccolo. "I know you care deeply for this wom — "

"I don't," Gabriel cut him off. "But I do feel responsible for her. I will find out who did this."

"We'll find out together," said Niccolo.

Kara, Niccolo's familiar padded out from one of the bedrooms and sat down at Niccolo's feet. Kara was a large brown and gold tabby cat that fed psychically from him. Where he was, she was not far behind.

Niccolo knelt, his thigh muscles flexing under his tight jeans, and scratched the cat behind the ear. It was jarring to see Niccolo — a consummate badass and frequent stalker and executioner of rogue Vampir — with the cat. The more Niccolo killed, the more he lost his soul.

Gabriel suspected Kara was there to aid in slowing that process. The cat had already helped Niccolo immensely, Gabriel assumed, in helping him retain what was left of his heart. Niccolo grew darker with every passing day and it worried Gabriel. But Niccolo would not agree to cease his work as executioner. He said it was the only thing he knew, and after centuries doing it, that may well have been true. After all, even before Niccolo had been Embraced, he'd been in the killing business.

"What the hell is going on up here?" said Charlie, walking down the hallway. "All the Demi are agitated."

Adam emitted a choked laugh. "You missed a great show." He sobered and flicked a look at Gabriel. "And I found out I'm being demoted. Not that I already didn't suspect it after that comment Gabe made tonight at the ball."

"No," Gabriel answered quickly. "I've reconsidered. You're getting a second chance. Things have changed since I made that decision, and I need you right now, Adam. I need everyone." He paused. "But you better get your little problem under control or you *will* be demoted soon. I can't afford to have someone who takes such stupid risks occupying such a high position in the management of this territory."

Gabriel understood the desire to take humans. It was what they were meant to do. The Embraced had evolved from humans originally, in order to combat a threat humans could not see, hear, or touch in their physical reality—not most of them, anyway. Necessity was the mother of invention and, in this case, the mother of evolution.

A race called the Dominion had feasted on the emotions of humans since the dawn of time, in some periods bringing man dangerously close to extinction. The Dominion did not reside in physical reality, but just outside of it, always looking for a way in. They worked primarily through dreams, feeding and sucking out the positive emotions from humans as they slept. A truly bad attack by the Dominion could leave a human man ready to kill himself by morning. Left unchecked, the Dominion could destroy the world while they sated their incredible hunger.

The humans didn't understand this, though they'd been told numerous times. They tended not to believe what they couldn't see, touch, taste or feel. And since the Dominion didn't reside in this vibrational level of reality, but in the next one, humans rarely remembered their encounters with them while they slept. They only felt the fatigue, the depression, the subtle slivering off of a piece of their soul, in the aftermath of a Dominion's attack. They didn't understand the symbiotic triad between the Dominion, the Embraced and humankind. The Embraced fought and suppressed the Dominion for the humankind. In turn, the Embraced fed from humans. It was a balance.

But no longer.

Politics, bureaucracy and fear had destroyed the equilibrium and endangered the world.

"Consider this a warning, Adam," finished Gabriel.

Adam let out a bark of laughter. "Yeah, right, a really badass warning. I *will* get this under control, Gabe. It's like an addiction, but I will. I promise."

"What happened?" asked Charlie again.

Gabriel filled him in.

"I'm sorry about the woman, Gabriel," said Charlie. "I hope she can fight through the Demi."

"It happens," said Niccolo. "Gabriel did it."

"Yes, but besides me, when's the last time you saw an unmarked human get through the Demi, Niccolo?" asked Gabriel.

Niccolo stood, after giving Kara one last scratch. "It's been a while, but I've seen it happen many times over the years. The odds are not in her favor, but that doesn't mean it's not possible."

A sweet, feminine scent wafted to the men, preceding an example of an unmarked human who could not fight through the Demi. Laila, a Demi who lived at Raven House, sauntered sexily down the hallway toward them. Her lithe, long body was encased in a nearly sheer lavender-colored negligee that displayed her full breasts, slim stomach, thighs and the patch of light hair between her legs. She wore her long blond hair loose and flipped over one shoulder so the curling tendrils brushed over a dark pink nipple as she walked. Laila was a breathtakingly beautiful woman.

She narrowed cat-shaped blue eyes at Gabriel. "You've come home, Gabriel," she purred. "You never come to the house these days." Her shapely lips formed a moue. "You never come to see me anymore."

Laila fancied herself in love with him. Gabriel had spent the last year trying to convince her she wasn't, that he wasn't the right man for her to pursue. He couldn't love back. Not a human. Not a Demi. Not another fully Embraced Vampir. No one. He could fuck well enough, but he couldn't give a woman his emotion.

Gabriel didn't understand her fixation on him. He was her *pere de sang*, blood father, and had Embraced her at her lover's request around two hundred years ago. Gabriel hadn't wanted to do it. However, she—along with Gabriel's friend and her lover, Xavier Alexander— had begged him.

Xavier had been marked and was newly Embraced at the time. He and Laila had been so much in love, they hadn't been able to stomach the idea of Laila growing old and dying while Xavier stayed young forever. Laila hadn't been strong enough to pass through the Demi stage, however, and in the several years that followed Xavier had watched Laila feed on many different people—male and female—in order to keep herself alive. It had been too much for Xavier and he'd committed suicide about six years after Laila had been Embraced.

Even though Laila and Xavier had known the risks, and Gabriel had argued long and hard against it, Gabriel felt he owed Laila something for giving in and Embracing her, for committing her to an existence of feeding from sex.

She sidled up to him and wound a cool arm through his. "Stay the night," she pouted. "Say you will. I've missed you." She leaned forward and pressed her breasts to his arm. "You never stay with me these days."

He disentangled himself. "I can't, Laila. I have things to do."

"A woman," she said softly, looking away.

Christ, he didn't want to hurt her, but it seemed inevitable. "Yes, but not in the way you think."

Charlie stepped forward. "I'll take care of you tonight, Laila."

Laila looked from Charlie to Gabriel. Her lower lip quivered. "But I want Gabriel."

Charlie flicked a glance at Gabriel and gave a sad half-smile. "Well, I guess you'll have to *settle* for me." He wound his arm around her waist and led her down the hallway.

Laila cast a long, lingering look back at Gabriel that made him want to groan. How she'd developed that silly emotional attachment to him, he didn't understand. Perhaps it was the old link between himself and Xavier?

Gabriel pushed a hand through his hair. "I need to get back in case Fate wakes up."

"I talked with Samantha," said Niccolo. "They're taking samples at the scene of the attack. Maybe that can provide us with some clues. I'll call and tell them that Fate has been found. They will likely want to come and get a statement from her sometime tomorrow. You're keeping her at your house?"

Gabriel nodded. Human hospitals had never mastered the art of medical care for the Embraced—not that they needed it very often. He would take care of Fate himself.

"I told Samantha to keep the investigation quiet, but I don't know if she'll have much control over that."

Gabriel grimaced. Usually it leaked. He knew all too well it would be splashed over the newspapers one day soon. Humanity couldn't get enough of the sensational exploits of the Vampir. Not since the battle of 1890 in New York City when the Embraced had battled the Dominion. Even though the conflict had occurred in the middle of the night in deepest winter, and in an unpopulated part of town to boot, several prominent New York businessmen who'd been passing through in their carriage had spotted them. They'd gone to the press, and had started a countrywide fervor for spotting paranormal activity. A few publicity-seeking Vampir later, and the Embraced's cover had been blown. Nothing had been the same since.

"I would like Dorian Cross thoroughly checked into. I want to know everything there is to know about him," said Gabriel to Niccolo.

"I know he's completely human."

"He appears to be. I don't smell any Vampir in him, but just because he's human doesn't mean he's harmless.

He's taken a huge interest in Fate and I'd like to know why. Maybe it's because he enjoys her paintings…maybe not. Maybe he has a motive for wanting Fate to become Embraced. Maybe even for putting her in my way. We won't know until we investigate."

"I'll pull the files on him from when he first started taking an interest in her a couple years back. This time, I'll build on them, go deeper and farther," answered Niccolo.

"I'm going to get Mihail to fly to Dallas to watch Drayden Lex. Mihail is in New York right now, but I'm sure, considering his own history with Dray, he won't mind doing this for us."

Niccolo twisted his lips in a bitter smile. "Drayden."

"He's been after this territory for years and our personal feud is centuries old. He'd have a reason to want me occupied and emotionally distracted if he were brewing up some plot to unseat me as keeper and increase his own area."

"Definitely," answered Niccolo. Niccolo had his own history with the egomaniac Drayden Lex. Drayden had made a lot of dangerous enemies over the centuries.

"It might be for nothing." Gabriel frowned. "After all, how would he know I'd been keeping watch on Fate, or that she meant anything to me?"

Niccolo gave a low laugh. "*Dio*, Gabriel. Anyone who ever watched you watch her would know. It was obvious from the beginning there was something about her you liked and that sentiment only grew the more time you spent monitoring her activities."

Gabriel shook his head. "It's true I was very drawn to her, but I highly doubt that anyone would read that kind of false emotion into it."

"False emotion?" Niccolo gave a rusty-sounding bark of laughter, turned and walked toward the stairs. Kara followed at his heels. "You, my friend, are blind in many ways. I will go now and start my investigation of Dorian Cross."

Gabriel watched him leave. Most of the Demi had filtered back downstairs now that the excitement was over.

Many of the older Embraced—Demi and Vampir alike—had amassed wealth over the years through the sale of antiques, appreciation on property and other investments. In reality, much of the world's wealth lay in old Vampiric and Demi hands. He also had much money, both in cold hard cash and property. He employed quite a few of the Embraced to manage his affairs and see to the running of his territory.

The fact that he was keeper earned him a spot on the Council of the Embraced, a much-coveted position of power. If you kept more than one territory, you retained two seats on the council and more power in the decision-making within Embraced policy and law. It was not unlike the board the directors of a large company. The council also paid the keepers a nice income to enforce laws and policies.

Gabriel had never sought anything more than one territory and one seat on the council. Drayden Lex, however, sought more than his fair share. Having a man like Drayden with that much power was distasteful. Lex was ethically impaired to say the least, and dealings in his territory were rife with shadiness. And Lex had always expressed an interest in acquiring Gabriel's holdings—no matter where they lay. That Gabriel's current territory lay next to his was only further incentive.

Gabriel walked back downstairs and out the front door of Raven House. The Demi on the first floor whispered as he passed, but he didn't pay attention to them. He was far too busy compiling a list of suspects in his head, all the individuals who would possibly want to see Fate as a Vampir or a Demi.

On his way home, he swung by Fate's apartment to pick up some of her belongings.

No matter what she woke up as, Demi or Vampir, she would have to stay with him for a while, until he felt her life was not in danger. Until they found the bastards who'd attacked her.

Rain falling from the night-black sky pattered against the stained glass windows running the tops of the walls of her living room. It'd been a church before they'd renovated it into studio apartments. A kitchen and dining area lay to his left.

She'd done the place in different shades of blue, her favorite color. Her futon stood in the center of the room, still unmade. Her down comforter lay in a big fluffy blob in the center of the mattress, the sheets twisted around it.

Gabriel knew she did odd things in her sleep. Even more so, in the past year. Twisting, turning and kicking. *Fighting.* Gabriel had slipped into her apartment many times to watch her sleep. He'd also found her in the realm of dream and observed her abilities with the Dominion.

It was one of the reasons he'd watched her so closely for so long. Fate had the interesting ability of being able to pass into the nether realm when she slept, to regain her sense of self and become aware of her surroundings. Her psychic ability extended even into her dream-self. She could locate the Dominion there and fight with them.

Gabriel knew how interested the Dominion were in her, and that made the Vampir interested in her as well.

The bathroom was a mess, presumably from her haste at getting ready for the ball. Gabriel ran his hand over the open cosmetic containers and sniffed the sweet scent of the perfume that still hung in the air.

He walked back out into the main room. Her easel sat in the center of the living room, a pink throw rug on the hardwood floor in front of it. Canvases stood everywhere, propped against the bed, the kitchen table and practically every wall.

He picked up the easel and the painting that stood half-finished on it and put them in his SUV. He also collected her paints, some clothing and toiletries, her childhood teddy bear…and one of the three handguns she owned. Then he locked her apartment door and headed back home.

When Gabriel arrived, he checked Fate before anything else and found her still unconscious. He went back downstairs and unloaded her things from the car, then returned to his bedroom.

Fate lay on her side with one hand curled against the pillow. It appeared she slept, but Gabriel knew her body was doing far more than that. Fate still shivered despite the heavy blankets covering her.

Gabriel looked down, realizing he still wore his tuxedo. He stripped, leaving only his pants on, climbed into the bed and pulled Fate close to him.

She turned toward him, seeking and snuggling into his body heat, and ran her fingers through the dark hair on his chest. Gabriel's whole body tensed at the feel of her hand on his skin. She shifted, sliding one long bare leg over his thigh to settle between his legs.

He gritted his teeth. *Christ.*

He cursed the fact he'd left his pants on. He wanted to feel her creamy skin against his. She snuggled closer, pressing her breasts against his side. Gabriel's cock hardened for her.

She shivered one last time, gave a small sigh and went still. Gabriel rested his chin on the top of her head and closed his eyes.

For rest of the night, he stayed that way, content to have her in his arms.

* * * * *

Fate roused and opened her eyes. She was enveloped in warmth and strength, lying embraced in someone's arms, her head cushioned on a chest that felt both hard and soft at the same time. Blurriness clouded her vision. She blinked twice and an overstuffed blue chair came into view. Glancing around, she took in the rest of her surroundings.

Cream-colored carpet and walls.

The entrance to a large walk-in closet.

The door leading to what looked like an enormous bathroom.

Where the hell was she? And, more importantly, who the hell was she in bed with?

Fate moved her head and saw Gabriel Letourneau's gorgeous face, his eyes closed in slumber. She pushed up from his silk and steel chest...and that's when it all hit her.

Chapter Three

"*Oh…my…God,*" she breathed. Her head pounded out a staccato rhythm, almost as hard as her heart. She felt different, weakened, as though she hadn't slept for two days and, oddly, at the same time, she felt stronger than she ever had in her life.

The night before came back in series of nightmarish flashes. She remembered the carjacking and fighting with the two men. Then she remembered the hooded man who'd bitten her. She remembered the taste of blood on her tongue.

And how much she'd liked it.

It hadn't tasted metallic, like she would've thought. It had been rich, like aged wine, and frighteningly addictive.

Then she'd been dumped unceremoniously on someone's front porch. She'd tried to get up and walk away, but she hadn't been able to move much. Then the flow of knowledge had begun. Information had slammed into her mind like some computer with an ultra-fast connection had been plugged into the back of her head to download file after file. Now she knew so many things she hadn't before. About the Vampir. About an ancient, highly malevolent race called the Dominion. She already knew them, she'd realized. They were the ones she fought on the other side.

She'd also known what was happening to her. Known her attacker had *Embraced* her.

Fate had been familiar with the Embraced before her attack. Everyone knew about them. They were fascinating, and oddly compelling to humans. Hated by some, loved by others, worshipped by a few.

Now she knew the details that humankind didn't know, and knew them like she was one of them. But she *wasn't* one of them, so what was going on? She couldn't be one of them...*right*? Although, if she'd been Embraced, then it only went to follow that...

No.

Her mind shut down on the possibility. It simply couldn't be.

She groaned, flipped the blankets back and looked around.

Gabriel Letourneau lay beside her, fast asleep. The sight of him caused her body to tighten instantly in oddly misplaced sexual awareness. Now was hardly the time, but she couldn't seem to help herself.

His black dress pants were slung low on his hips, the top button undone. His powerful chest with its golden skin was shirtless, and he'd thrown one arm up over his head in a position that defined his biceps. Smooth muscle rippled over the expanse of his chest and arms. A light dusting of dark chest hair tapered into a treasure trail that went down his stomach, past the waistband of his pants. She thought about where that trail led and a hard, hot flush overcame her body.

Her gaze found the pulse in his throat and lingered there. Hunger started low in her belly and spread out. She imagined peeling his pants off and stroking his cock, taking it into her mouth, against her tongue. She envisioned him rolling her over and impaling her with it, shafting her slow at first and then faster and harder. She imagined his muscled body working above her, his breathing harsh and arousing in her ear.

She'd bite his throat as they came together and satisfy all her desires at once.

She stared hard at his pulse and her mouth watered.

His blue eyes opened, then widened. "Fate." He rose onto one elbow and stared at her. "Are you all right?"

"I-I, uh, don't know. I feel strange."

"What do you want right now? Sex or blood?"

She stared at his lips, tracing them with her gaze and wanting to taste them. She imagined him rolling her back into the pillows and settling that luscious mouth over her nipples, trailing them down to her pussy and licking her until she screamed in climax. Yesterday, the last thing on her mind had been sex. It hadn't been something she'd wanted in a long time. Now it was all she seemed able to think of.

She looked up from his lips. "Sex," she said thickly.

His eyes instantly darkened with what Fate knew had to be arousal. "*Mon Dieu*," he murmured. He sat up and drew her toward him.

Her pussy flooded with moisture at the feel of his hands on her, the slide of her bare skin against his. That's when she realized what she wore—only her bra and thong. That knowledge only served to excite her more.

What was *wrong* with her? Had she turned into some raging nymphomaniac overnight?

Gabriel pulled her over him, so she straddled his waist, then slid his hand to the nape of her neck and pressed her mouth down to his throat. "Rub your lips against my skin, *ma cheri*. Feel the veins pulsing, the blood rushing through them. Inhale the scent of my life force. Imagine what it would be like to consume it, what it would taste like."

She rubbed her mouth against his sleep-warmed throat, feeling stubble scrape against the tender flesh of her lips and inhaling the remnants of his heady cologne. Fate laid a kiss to his skin and flicked her tongue out to taste him. Beneath her, Gabriel tensed. His cock hardened, pressing up against her sex through his pants.

She could smell his blood, the exquisitely aged liquor pulsing through his veins. Hunger curled through her stomach, shot up her spine and out, overwhelming her body, overwhelming even her desire for sex. Her incisors shifted and extended down into small points.

Her breath came heavy and her heart pounded. Reality slammed home. Heaven above, she was a Vampir. And worse...

She was hungry.

She scraped her fangs over his flesh, seeking, searching for a way in, unsure of how to proceed.

"Ah, yes," he breathed, seeming relieved. "I feel your fangs." Gabriel's hands closed around the bare skin of her waist. "You made it through." The words came out thankful and slightly surprised. He gave a short little laugh.

She shifted on him, grinding her pussy down on him slowly, feeling the hard length of his cock press against her. He was very impressive, she noted, and highly aroused.

Her movement earned her a sexy rumbling groan from Gabriel. "Don't tease me, *ma cheri*, just bite me."

Fate sunk her fangs into his skin and found a flow of blood to pull on. She closed her eyes in ecstasy. The thick blood tasted hot and spicy and just a little bit sweet. It filled her, giving her body what it craved, what it needed.

"Yes," Gabriel hissed. His hips stabbed up against her. Fate cursed the clothing that separated them as he ground against her slowly, in a teasing semblance of the actual act.

She pressed her hands to his chest, feeling the hard, warm muscles flexing as he wrapped his arms around and stroked her skin. Teasingly, he ran his thumb under the small scrap of the thong at the small of her back.

He moved his other hand up and undid her bra clasp. Her breasts spilled from the lacey cups and he caught them. Taking them in his large hands, he massaged them and worked the nipples between his fingers and brushed back and forth over them with the pads of his thumbs.

Oh…yes…

She pulled away from him, releasing his throat. Her pussy was wet and plumped with excitement. Fate couldn't remember the last time she'd been so aroused. It was as though her body was not her own.

She ran her fingers over his chest, feeling his defined pectorals and then trailing around each of his nipples. He shuddered and closed his eyes. Fate leaned forward, pressed her lips to his, and traced around them with the tip of her tongue.

Suddenly, she found herself flat on her back beneath him. His mouth slanted over hers and he plunged his tongue within to savagely tangle with hers. Her breasts rubbed against his chest, stealing her breath and her thought.

He inserted a knee between her thighs and forcibly parted them. Settling himself between them, he pressed his cock against the tender, aroused folds of her pussy and thrust so she could feel how hard he was. God, she hated that he still wore his pants. Her thong would be so easy to get around.

Fate moaned into his mouth and arched up against him. She ran her hands over his bare back and shoulders, feeling his muscles tense and bunch when he moved.

He broke the kiss, grabbed her wrists and pinned them to the bed on either side of her. Sexual heat emanated from his heavy-lidded eyes. "Don't touch me, Fate. I cannot be responsible for what will happen if you do. You are in the throes of the Embrace, right now. Your mind is clouded and your body demands things your will doesn't necessarily desire. I would not want you to regret something later that we did now. I don't want to be a regret to you."

But, oh, how she needed a release. She moved her hips against him. "Please, I need—"

"I know what you need, *ma cheri*. I will not let you suffer." He released her wrists.

"What's wrong with me? Normally I'm not at all—"

"It's an effect of the Embrace. It will last for a while, but will lessen in degree. At first it overwhelms everything else." His gaze slid to her breasts and her nipples responded instantly. "Let me ease your discomfort."

His voice was a silken rasp moving over her skin. She licked her lips. "Yes."

He shifted to her side and took a nipple into his warm mouth. Gently, he pulled on it, traced it with his tongue, and alternately sucked on it like it was a piece of candy.

He smoothed his hand down over her stomach and circled her clit through the damp material of her thong. Then he moved down, teasing her labia with his fingertips through the thin strip of fabric of her thong.

"Gabriel," she breathed, closing her eyes. Her body was so ready to climax.

He moved, pulling the tiny scrap of material over her hips, down her legs and off. For a long moment there was no sound, no movement. Fate opened her eyes.

Gabriel knelt on the bed beside her. His eyes were hooded, darkened. Sexual heat radiated from his body, warming her. His gaze traveled over her at leisure and she nearly came right then from the look in his eyes.

His gaze settled on her face. "God, you're beautiful." Almost imperceptibly, his voice shook.

She smiled. Fate couldn't remember a time a man had said that to her and sounded so sincere.

He reached down and rubbed her thigh. "Spread your legs for me, Fate," he purred in a velvet voice.

She complied and he moved between them. He slicked his finger through her cream and used it as lubricant around her swollen and sensitive clit. He circled around it with his finger until Fate moaned. It wasn't enough to make her come, just enough to drive her to the edge and keep her there.

"Do you like it, *ma cheri*?"

She closed her eyes and nodded, losing herself in sensation.

"So do I," he said. "I enjoy watching your face, hearing your breath hitch and your moans and little cries. Do you want to come?"

"Yes," she gasped.

Gabriel leaned over her, bracing himself on one hand, and placed his mouth to her breast. He flicked his tongue over her nipple as he thrust two fingers in and out of her pussy.

Fate cried out, reveling in the magic he wove over her body. He nipped at her nipple with his teeth and she nearly came undone.

He moved, perhaps sensing she was near climax, and kissed his way down the length of her body, pausing once to taste her belly button. He ran the tip of his tongue through the hair covering her mound and lapped at her clit.

"Oh, yes," she cried.

His finger found her anus and circled it, teasing the nerve endings there. "What about here, *ma cheri?* Do you enjoy it when a man loves you here?"

She'd never had a man take her there, though she'd always been curious, had fantasized about it on numerous occasions. "I-I don't know," she breathed.

"Hmmm…we will find that out later, yes?"

"Anything you want to do to me," she moaned. "Anything."

"I like the sound of that word coming from your lips." He laid a kiss to her inner thigh, followed by a quick lick. Gabriel shifted, laved over her labia and thrust his tongue into her. She reared up, pressing her swollen pussy into his face. His finger traced around and around her anus like a dark promise. He half groaned, half growled into her aroused, damp flesh, vibrating her.

Oh, God. She was going to go mad.

"Gabriel, please, I need you."

He didn't answer. Instead, he latched his mouth over her clit and slipped his fingers back into her pussy. He pumped her hard and fast, just like how she wanted his cock. His fingertips found and rasped over her G-spot skillfully, making her buck her hips. Fate writhed and panted as he laved and sucked her clit. All the while, he groaned as if she was the best thing he'd ever tasted.

Fate came undone and she climaxed harder than she ever had in her life. Spasms of pleasure shook her body like they never had before. She cried out under the force of them. Using his hands and tongue, he drew her orgasm out until her vision darkened and she thought she'd pass out.

Slowly, he brought her down, gentling her with small caresses and kisses. He licked over her pussy with the flat of his tongue as though he couldn't get enough of the taste of her. Then he pulled away and collapsed on the bed beside her.

Fate's breathing slowly returned to normal and she noted how his cock strained against the material of his pants. She turned toward him and reached out to stroke it. "But what about y —"

He had her wrist before she could make contact. "Fate, if you touch me even once right now, I will disgrace myself in a very expensive pair of pants. You have no idea how much I want you," he finished through gritted teeth.

She leaned back against the pillows. "Then take me. I'm yours."

He sighed. "If you say that again later today, after these initial reactions to the Embrace have passed, you'll be mine, Fate. Every last luscious inch of you will be answering to me, and you had better be ready for it."

She shivered at his words, still feeling the residual effects of her body's recent carnal demands, even though the sexual spell that had held sway over her since she'd awoken was starting to wear off now that her body had gotten what it needed. Gabriel had softened the sharp edge of it with his blood and the climax he'd bestowed upon her.

Now the incredible darkness of what had happened to her finally began to register. A sick feeling settled in the pit of her stomach.

She leaned her head back, swallowed hard and closed her eyes. "I'm no longer human."

"You're Embraced now, Fate. You're a fully Embraced Vampir."

Tears pricked her eyes and choked her throat. Last night, her life had been normal. Last night, she'd almost been happy. In a flash all that had changed...*she'd* been changed. She opened her eyes and blinked back the tears. "Who did this to me, Gabriel?" she whispered.

Gabriel swung his feet over the edge of the bed and stood. "I don't know, but I'll find out. When I do, they will pay."

Fate pulled the blankets over her nude body, suddenly feeling exposed and more than a little vulnerable. "Why would anyone want to Embrace me against my will?"

Gabriel ran a hand through his hair. "Again, I don't know."

Her eyes narrowed. "And how are you involved?"

"You mean, why did you end up on my front porch?" He paused. "I believe someone meant to use you to hurt me."

"Why? I don't mean anything to you. We only first met last night. Yes, you like my paintings. And, yes, you were definitely trying to woo me into your bed last night, and I would have gone willing, perhaps even pursued you, but I don't mean anything to you personally or emotionally."

Gabriel went still and stared at her for several heartbeats. "There's something more I have to tell you. You met me for the first time last night. I, on the other hand, have known you much longer."

Her brow furrowed. "What do you mean?"

He sat down beside her on the bed. "It came to my attention five years back, when I first took over this territory, that you were special."

"Special?"

"Fate, you've known were different since you were child, haven't you?"

She shifted uncomfortably. It was a painful subject for her. Psychic ability had dominated her life almost since it had begun. As a child, she hadn't known to hide her abilities, hadn't know that they would threaten and frighten others. The result had been rejection by her peers. That's what had driven her to become an artist. She'd thrown herself into her painting when the other children had teased her and pushed her away. It had been an enjoyable escape and a way for her to express her emotions when there had been no one to talk to. "Yes," she answered carefully.

"You've always had an active night life, haven't you, Fate? I don't mean the social kind. You've always known when you were dreaming and have been able to control those dreams. Isn't that right? You've been able to retain your sense of self and travel."

"Yes."

"When I discovered you purely by accident one night while I was dreamwalking, I knew you'd be of acute interest to the Dominion. Humans with your level of ability are very rare. So I've been watching you for five years closely, to make sure they didn't target you in any way or use you somehow to their advantage."

Fate swallowed hard. The Dominion were the bogeymen of dreamland. "I've fought them on numerous occasions when traveling over there."

"I know. I've watched you do it." He reached out and cupped her cheek in his hand. Slowly, he rubbed his thumb back and forth over her bottom lip. "I know a lot of things about you. I've invested a lot of time and energy in you—watching you, protecting you."

She grabbed his wrist, stilling his movement. "So, if an enemy of yours knew this, they may have decided I really *do* mean something to you."

"Yes."

Rage bubbled up within her. She bolted from the bed, unmindful of her nudity, and whirled on him. "I didn't want to be Embraced and I don't want to be Vampir." Lightheadedness suddenly racked her, bowing her knees.

Gabriel caught her before she collapsed. "But you *were* Embraced, Fate. You *are* Vampir. I'm sorry, but those are the realities."

"Why do I feel so weak?"

"Your very DNA was altered. Even for someone with a mark — someone meant to become Vampir — the Embrace is highly draining. For a person without a mark, it's downright dangerous. You're lucky you made it through the Demi phase at all. You'll be weak for a while."

Yeah, and horny too, Fate thought. Already her body tightened again in desire just from having Gabriel's arms around her.

She struggled to her feet and pushed away from him. Spying the sheet on the bed, she grabbed it and wrapped it around herself. A long mirror hung on the back of the bathroom door. She padded across the hardwood floor to it and examined her reflection. A bruise decorated her cheek. Gingerly, she touched it and winced. "Everything happened so fast, I don't even remember receiving this."

"You had other injuries, but they healed as a result of the Embrace. That one was particularly bad, but it looks better than it did last night. By this evening, it will likely be healed."

"Bastards," she murmured. Her body hummed with impotent rage. She wanted to lash out, take revenge, but she had no one to go after. She wanted to cry, kick, scream, but that would do no good, serve no purpose. All she had the strength for at the moment was numb acceptance and the deep depression of anger turned inward.

She turned. "I need to get home, Gabriel. Will you take me?"

He shook his head. "You must stay here. Where I can protect you."

Fate fought the urge to scream. "I can take care of myself," she bit off.

"Remember last night, Fate? A human, even a black belt in Tae Kwon Do, is no match for a Vampir."

"I'm no longer human, Gabriel," she snapped.

He shook his head again. "True, but you're not seasoned Embraced, either. You are too weak, Fate. You will stay here. I don't know yet what we're dealing with. I don't know if they'll come after you again or not. I need to be able to protect you."

She set her jaw. "I need my canvases, my paints. It's how I cope with stress."

"I understand that. I have already taken the liberty of bringing some things from your apartment, your easel and paints, some clothing, and other items."

"Of course," she said bitterly. She walked toward him, holding the sheet against her body. "Because you know where my apartment is and how to get in without a key, and you know everything I'd want to pack down to the shade of eye shadow, wouldn't you?"

Gabriel only nodded.

"So my *stalker* of five years knows me well." She narrowed her eyes. "But I don't know *him* at all."

"I am sorry for this situation, Fate. I don't know what else to say." He walked to the door. "Take a bath. Take a nap. Rest. Give yourself time to accept what has happened. Then come downstairs. Your canvasses and paints are there." He stepped into the hallway. "I will be but a thought away should you need me."

* * * * *

Gabriel closed the door and headed down the hallway.

It wasn't easy for her to stay here, but it wasn't easy for him to have her here, either. After all, he hadn't directly cohabitated with a woman in over 369 years. He was a little out of practice.

Gabriel always made sure that after he bedded a woman, either he or she was gone shortly thereafter. Now he had one in his house, sleeping in his bed, taking baths in his tub, breathing the same air. Being domestic.

It was going to be damned disconcerting.

He headed into the guest bedroom where he kept some clothes. After grabbing a pair of jeans and a shirt, he entered the bathroom, started the shower and stripped his pants and boxers off.

And, *Christ*, he wanted her.

He'd barely been able to hang on as he'd brought her to climax. He'd wanted so much to sink his cock into her warm, tight pussy. She'd been so sweet, so wet. It had been a supreme act of restraint not to climb up her luscious body and thrust his cock inside her when she'd begged for him.

One thing was certain; he'd make sure she begged for him again when she wasn't under the thrall of the Embrace. He wouldn't restrain himself then. When that time came, and she pleaded with him to give it to her hard and fast, he'd honor her request with pleasure.

He stepped into the shower and groaned as the hot water sluiced down his body. Gabriel picked up the soap and lathered it over his chest. His cock went hard with only the thought of her. He could taste the cream of her sex in his mouth, could feel the muscles of her pussy as he'd sunk his fingers into her. Her small clit had felt so sweet against his tongue.

He set the bar of soap down, leaned one hand against the wall of the shower and took his soaped cock in his other. Working his hand up and down on his straining erection, he gripped himself as tightly as he imagined Fate's pussy would. He'd fuck her slow and easy in the beginning. Her sex would hold him, the muscles rippling around his shaft as he glided in and out of her with deliberate slowness. Fate would writhe beneath him, calling his name. She'd beg him to take her harder, deeper.

His hand tightened at the thought and his cock jerked. He stroked himself faster, imagining how Fate would moan as he picked up the pace of his thrusts. He'd shift his hips, angling so the head of his cock brushed her G-spot.

Her eyes would darken with mindless passion as she looked up at him. Her mouth would slacken in ecstasy. Her body would tense, shudder, and then she would break apart beneath him in sweet release. The muscles of her pussy would convulse and ripple, pulling at his shaft. She would drench him with her come and his cock would drink up every last bit of it.

Gabriel came on a hoarse shout, his cock jumping in his hand as a stream of come shot from it. His breathing harsh, he leaned against the wall of the shower and closed his eyes. What had pushed him over the edge more than anything else had been look of emotion he'd imagined in her eyes. *Love.*

God, he was in trouble.

He rinsed and got out. After toweling himself off, he laid down on the guest bed with a weary groan. He could use a little sleep, too. Gabriel closed his eyes and took a minute to set up an energy field around the house. If anyone disturbed it beyond those people he'd invited into his home, he would know.

Without warning, an image of a blonde with sparkling blue eyes entered his mind.

Caroline.

He hadn't thought of her in years, but Gabriel's heart clenched nonetheless. She'd been the only woman he'd ever really loved. He'd had centuries to deal with the loss of her, and he had, but the memory of her could still dredge up deep pain.

Fate reminded him of Caroline. He'd noticed the similarities in their characters soon after he'd begun watching her. They were both strong, stubborn, and generous. They both painted and used their art as a way to interpret their lives and emotions.

Gabriel squeezed his eyes shut in an effort to banish the image. Now was not the time to relive the past or wallow in painful thoughts and regrets. Why was he even thinking of her? He tried to shift his thoughts in a different direction, but Caroline's image remained lodged in his mind, no matter how hard he tried to dissolve it.

The door opened and Caroline walked in, bundled in layers of clothing against the bitter winter weather. Gabriel stood and went to her.

"I did it, Gabriel!" she cried. "I sold the painting." She smiled up at him, her cheeks rosy and her blue eyes bright. She'd come from a local merchant's home, a man who'd admired her work and had expressed an interest in buying some of it.

He drew her against him and kissed her long and deep. Joy filled him. This was her very first sale in a climate that was openly hostile to women painters. "I'm so proud of you," he murmured against her lips.

He unwrapped each swathe of protective fabric, until her rounded belly was revealed. He pulled her to him and ran his palm over it.

Their first child.

Proud bliss filled him as he drew her against him and covered her lips with his.

Gabriel jerked himself up, unable to go any further in his memories. He rubbed his hand over his face and sighed. Did the pain of losing your wife and unborn child ever truly disappear? Perhaps not.

If Caroline had not contracted fever and died, taking their child along with her, Gabriel would likely never have been Embraced. His life would've been so much different. It would've ended centuries ago, but he would have been able to live it with the woman he loved most in the world, and he would've had a reflection of her always in his child's eyes.

For that, he would trade immortality if given the choice.

Instead, Caroline and the unborn babe had died, and Gabriel had nearly lost his mind in grief. He'd left their apartment with only one item, a small self-portrait of Caroline that he possessed to this day.

After that, he'd tried to slowly kill himself with alcohol. He'd been lying in an alley when Monia had found him. She'd brought him back to her *Auberge de Plaisir*, the house where her Demi lived. Gabriel lived there for years as "food" for the Demi, until one day he contracted the very same fever from which Caroline had died.

He'd wished for death, but Monia had foiled his efforts at it and Embraced him instead. To the surprise of all, he, an unmarked human, had passed through the Demi and obtained fully Embraced status.

At first Gabriel had hated Monia for what she'd done, but over the years he'd come to be grateful. These days Monia was one of his closest friends.

Gabriel lay back on the bed and tried to relax. It was a long time before he slept and when he finally did, his dreams were haunted by painful whispers of emotion from his past.

Chapter Four

Fate dabbed more paint on her brush and placed it to the canvas in front of her. She hadn't been able to sleep, though she had taken Gabriel's suggestion of a bath. The grief of losing her former life made her feel heavy and tired, and she'd sat in the warm water and stared into space for a long time as she processed recent events.

Anger. That was what had compelled her to get out of the tub and get dressed. That was what had driven her downstairs to pick up her paintbrush. That's the emotion that sustained her. Simmering rage flowed through her. Her veins seemed to hum with it.

But what was, *was*...and Fate had always been resilient. She would get through this as she'd survived so many other traumas in her life...and she *would* find her revenge against the person who'd done it. That goal was forefront in her mind.

That morning she'd explored her surroundings. Gabriel's house was old, probably dating from the early 1800s. Though, Fate mused, likely Gabriel didn't think it was so old. Fate knew how much money he had because of the magazine articles that had been written on him. The man was loaded, yet he'd decorated his home very simply and in a very masculine way. The floors were wood and mostly bare besides a few throw rugs scattered here and there. The furnishings and window hangings were all of different shades of green. His couch and chairs were overstuffed, inviting and comfortable-looking. There was no pretension in his house, despite his wealth. It was a *home*, pure and simple.

Her paintings hung on the walls of the house alongside other far older works. She'd spent most of the morning walking through the huge house, exploring them all. It was odd to see her paintings there, since each one was like a little a bit of her soul. Gabriel had pieces of her soul displayed within his house. It was an intimate and strangely pleasing revelation.

One of the stairs squeaked and she looked up from her work to see Gabriel descending. He was barefoot and wore an old pair of jeans. His chest was bare and he held a shirt in his hand. A surly expression marred his handsome face.

"Are you all right, Gabriel?" she asked when he didn't look at her or say anything.

He glanced at her and mumbled something unintelligible.

"Excuse me?"

"Didn't sleep well, disturbing dreams," he grumbled. He glanced at the table near her where she'd set her teddy bear, Mr. Jones. Her Glock lay in the bear's lap. "Teddy bear needs to defend himself?" he asked, frowning.

"Fate needs to defend herself. Teddy bear is holding the gun." She lowered her eyes and studied her canvas. "I'm sorry I snapped at you earlier."

"You have every reason to be angry, Fate. It's a normal reaction."

"It was a lot of revelations all at once. Too many. I-I need time to adjust."

"Of course."

"Thank you for bringing my gun and Mr. Jones."

He waved a hand. "Not a problem."

She turned toward him. "I-I remember you now. I remember you from my dreams. Sometimes when I traveled in them, you were there, watching me from the side. You were always shadowed, but your...*presence*...is familiar to me."

He ran a hand through his hair, and showed off his biceps as he did it. Did he *know* how gorgeous he was? "Yes, I watched you often while you slept, Fate. I knew that if the Dominion wanted to contact you, try to use you in some way, or harm you, it would be within that realm."

"On some level, I recognized you at the charity ball." She laughed. "I thought I was being crazy."

"Not crazy." He smiled. "Are you hungry?"

She looked at him with a blank expression.

"I mean for food. Our bodies don't need it, but it's still enjoyable to eat. And sometimes the newly Embraced have ghost hunger pangs. Sort of like an amputee who can still feel a limb even though it's gone."

"Oh." That was an interesting analogy. Her humanity had been amputated. She gave a heartfelt sigh and glanced at her painting. She was ruining it with her tenseness. "Yes, I do feel kind of hungry. The, uh, normal kind of hungry, that is." She set her brush down on her palette.

"The *sacyr* feels different than human hunger," he commented.

"The *sacyr*. That's what the Vampir call their hunger for blood, right? I got that from the information last night during the Embrace, but I also remember reading that about the Vampir — uh — before."

"Yes. A Vampir must never deny the *sacyr*. Especially not you, Fate."

"Especially not me? What do you mean by that?"

Gabriel paused. "Come into the kitchen. Let's sit and talk." He turned and headed down the hallway.

She stared after him, her face falling. Oh, *hell*. She couldn't take any more bad news. After pulling off her painting smock and setting it aside, she retrieved her Glock from Mr. Jones—she wasn't going anywhere without it from now on—and followed him down the hallway.

One of the old paintings that hung on the wall of the corridor that led to the kitchen caught her eye. She stopped to examine it. "Who is the boy in these paintings, Gabriel? He looks so much like you."

"It is me," called Gabriel from the kitchen.

She studied the painting. The boy had glossy black hair and long dark lashes. He was a beautiful child. One of those boys you could tell would grow into a gorgeous man. He'd had long hair even then. In the painting, he wore a hat to cover it, a pair of blue short breech-type leggings, a white shirt and blue jacket over it. He wore a sad expression on his face. Sorrowful emotion radiated out from his eyes.

After examining the boy's face for several long moments, she turned and walked into the kitchen. "How old are you, Gabriel?"

He set a glass down on the center island and looked at her. "I am 394 years old."

Her jaw dropped. She knew the Embraced were immortal, but she'd never truly *understood* what that meant until she'd become one. She, too, might live that long. "Don't you get bored with life?"

He laughed and reached for the full coffeepot. "Being an Embraced means you are never bored, *ma cheri*."

Suddenly speechless, Fate pulled up one of the stools at the center island and sat down. She placed her Glock on the table beside her, and glanced at the food he'd set out. Suddenly she didn't feel so hungry.

"Where were you born?" she asked.

"Bretagne. It is a region in France. I was a bastard child born to a very poor family. They sold me to be an artist's model when I was very young."

"That's terrible."

He chuckled. "It wasn't so bad. I've had an interesting life, at least. I will tell you the entire story sometime soon."

She glanced around the room. His kitchen was huge and sported stainless steel appliances and a large skylight in the middle of the room's ceiling. An island with an inset stove dominated the center. Above it hung a rack with copper pots and pans and a place where crystal wine and champagne glasses hung. An intimate breakfast nook stood to the left of the kitchen, in an alcove with a bay window that overlooked his green, rolling lawn. It was private yard, lined by tall, thick hedges and scattered throughout by mature trees.

"I'm still having trouble wrapping my mind around *394 years*," she commented.

"Fate, our life span is infinitely longer than a human's and that is a gift, not a curse. Your perspective will adjust. You'll soon see that an Embraced expects to live forever. It is normal to us. Just as a human expects to live to be only eighty-five or ninety years old."

"How can you kill an Embraced?" she asked suddenly. She didn't even know where the question had come from, save she'd been thinking of mortality. "I mean I know about the hawthorn. Everyone knows that. But since I'm now an Embraced myself, having a hawthorn stake or baton around doesn't really sound appealing. How else can you do it?"

Gabriel pulled up a stool beside her and sat down. "In all the regular ways you can kill a human, you just have to try ten times as hard."

She glanced at her Glock. "Will a bullet do it?"

He shrugged. "It depends where you hit the Vampir and how many times."

Fate narrowed her eyes. "Where's the best place to hit?"

"The head or the heart. A Vampir might be hard-pressed to heal multiple head or heart wounds. Though when I say *multiple*, I mean it." He glanced at the Glock. "How many rounds does it fire? Seventeen?"

"Yes."

"You'd have to empty it."

Fate looked away and shuddered. "Good to know." She drew a breath and looked back at him. "Okay, why do I, more than others, need to be sure and feed the *sacyr*?"

"You know firsthand how powerful the Dominion are, Fate. You've got psychic ability and were of mere interest to them as a human. Now that you're Embraced, you'll be a target. You will be too powerful for them to ignore. And if you do not feed the *sacyr*, you will be vulnerable to them."

"Why would they want to target me?"

"You will be a powerful dreamwalker as a Vampir, Fate. Combined with your psychic abilities, you will be able to hunt them down and destroy them easily."

She took a deep breath. *Oh, good.*

"I know of one other Vampir whom the Dominion targets specifically. Her name is Penelope and she is one of the strongest of us. She is able to sniff out the Dominion who have taken over human bodies."

Fate looked up in surprise. "I thought the Dominion possessing humans was only a myth."

"Oh, no. It can happen. As far as we know, it only occurs when the veil of energy that protects our realm from theirs grows thin. It is not often. Penny is on constant alert for the Dominion, but not even she has the same dreamwalking ability you will have. You'll be a real threat to them."

"Great." She laughed. "Well, at least I'll be good at something."

Gabriel gestured at the cold chicken and cheese on the table. "Eat. The food will not give you direct nourishment, but it is good for you psychologically."

Her gaze roved over his bare chest, tracing the hard, lean musculature of his biceps, pecs and abs. Lord, he was gorgeous. His hair was swept over one shoulder and fell nearly to his belly button. She couldn't help but remember how all that hair had felt brushing over her skin. Hardly knowing she did it, she reached out and ran her hand over his chest, stopping to play with one of his nipples. "I'm not hungry for food anymore," she murmured.

Sexual heat flared instantly in Gabriel's eyes. He slid off the stool, grabbed her wrist and pulled her forward, flush up against him. He pushed her against the counter and pressed his hips into her stomach, so she could feel his erection. He twined a hand through her hair and lowered his mouth to hers. "You tempt me beyond belief," he murmured against her lips. "And I have not fed yet today."

Suddenly, she wondered what being bitten by a Vampir would be like. Not in violence and anger as her attacker had done, but in sexual lust. They said it was orgasmic, an experience unparalleled by any other. There were humans who were addicted to it.

With firm yet gentle pressure he pulled her hair, and with it her head, and exposed the long line of her throat. He lowered his mouth to the expanse of vulnerable flesh and brushed his lips against her, right under her earlobe. A hot flash of arousal ripped through her, settling between her legs.

His breathing grew ragged and hers hitched as he continued the agonizingly slow glide of his lips down her neck. "I know your innermost desires, Fate," he murmured. "I know your darkest sexual fantasies. I know what you imagine when you use your vibrator. What forbidden sexual acts you play out in your mind to make yourself come."

She closed her eyes. Her pussy drenched at his words. He'd been in her subconscious mind, of course he knew. She supposed she should feel outraged, violated, but oddly she didn't. She only felt excited.

He kissed the place where her throat and shoulder met. "I'm going to make them all come true," he murmured with silken menace. He worked his way back up to her mouth and rubbed her lips with his. "Every." He licked at her upper lip. "Last." He nibbled her bottom lip. "One." His mouth slanted hard and hungry over hers, demanding she open to him. He slid his tongue within to tangle with hers. Gabriel did not merely kiss; he claimed her mouth. He nipped, licked and tasted, alternating with the hot, deep penetration of his tongue.

A whimper of need escaped her throat and she gripped his shoulders, kissing him back. She dipped a hand down to rub at his erection from the outside of his jeans. Her pussy felt so empty now. She wanted him within her.

He growled low in his throat and thrust against her palm. A series of images filled her mind, sent by Gabriel. In her mind's eye she saw him peeling her clothes off and lifting her onto the counter, unbuttoning his jeans and sliding them down far enough to free his cock. Images filled her mind of him yanking her ass to the edge of the counter and sliding his cock home, filling her so exquisitely, stretching her muscles as they'd never been stretched. He'd plunge in and out of her so hard and so fast that she wouldn't be able to think, barely be able to breathe.

He slid his warm hand down her stomach to her pussy. She spread her thighs for him and he ran his fingers over the ridge of her jeans that sat snugly against her sex, found her clit and rubbed little circles over it. The material of her jeans that separated them was frustrating, yet arousing at the same time. He circled it and circled it with his fingertip, applying just enough pressure to make her moan against his mouth.

She grasped the countertop behind her and thrust her hips up against him. Her breath came hard and fast now, and she tipped her head back, breaking the kiss. "Gabriel," she breathed. She'd done it as an open invitation and he took it.

He pressed his body closer to hers as his mouth came down on the long line of throat she offered him. His hand never left the apex of her thighs. He never stopped the perfectly pressured rotation of his finger around her clit as he brushed his lips over her sensitive skin and ran his teeth over it in a gesture that made her shiver with anticipation.

"I cannot," he murmured. "Not yet." He kissed her throat and pressed harder on her clit, circled it once, twice, and she came apart. Intense pleasure rocketed through her so hard it made her knees weak. He held her upright and covered her mouth with his, consuming the sounds of her climax.

Fate broke the kiss and gasped. "Oh my God," she murmured in amazement. Her hands moved to the buttons of his jeans, undoing them with fumbling motions. She finally freed his cock and stroked it. It was long and thick and as gorgeous as he was. It was thickly veined and had a large, suckable head. She wanted to run her tongue up its length and feel Gabriel's body tense and tremble. She wanted to suck it like a lollipop until he groaned. She wanted to make him crazy with her lips and tongue.

She knelt, suddenly needing to taste it.

"*Mon Dieu, oui,*" he said on a groan.

The doorbell rang.

Gabriel let out a string of curses in French and some other language she didn't recognize.

"Ignore them," said Fate. "It's probably just a salesperson." She ran her fingers up the length of him, drawing an agonized groan from his throat.

His hands gripped her shoulders, and he let a frustrated-sounding hiss of breath escape. "No, it is probably the police."

The intrusion of reality was like being doused with cold water. She stood.

Gabriel adjusted himself, wincing as he managed his erection, and did up his jeans. "They are here to get a statement from you about last night."

She let out a long, shuddering sigh. "And I was doing such a lovely job of forgetting, too."

Gabriel put his hands to her shoulders. The heat from his palms bled through the material of her shirt and warmed her skin. "I know you don't want to relive this experience, but the police may be able to help us find out who attacked you. It is very necessary."

She bit her lip and nodded. "I know. I understand that."

"I'll accompany you."

"Okay."

Together they walked to the door and opened it. A pretty, tall, red-haired woman in plainclothes stood there alongside a uniformed officer. "Gabriel," she greeted icily. Her gaze shifted to Fate. "You must be Fate. I'm Detective Samantha Ripley. I head the Squad for Paranormal and Vampiric Activity here in Newville."

SPAVA. Fate had heard of them. She put her hand to the door and tapped her nail against the heavy wood. "Ordinarily I'd say it's nice to meet you, but…"

"I understand," answered Samantha. "You've been through a lot lately. Condolences on becoming Embraced," she said dispassionately. "All the same, we really need to talk to you." Her gaze flicked past her, into Gabriel's house and then back to Fate. "Down at the station would be more ideal, if that's agreeable to you."

She sighed in resignation. "Fine, let me get my coat."

* * * * *

Gabriel sat in the SPAVA offices in downtown Newville and tried not to cross the floor to where Fate sat, sling her over his shoulder, and walk out. It was painful to see and hear her recount the events from the night before. The only thing that kept him from whisking her out of the office and back into his car was that it seemed to be a catharsis for her. She needed to deal with what had happened and SPAVA needed the details. He couldn't intervene just because it hurt him to watch her go through it.

The room was small and done in neutral colors. Samantha and Fate sat across from each other at a small table. Niccolo stood nearby. The only other piece of furniture in the room, besides the chair he sat in, was a long table holding a coffeemaker, some cups, and a platter of pastries that had gone untouched by everyone in the room.

"So, you say that you know of no one who would want to see you punished for anything, Fate. You have no enemies at all?" asked Samantha.

Fate shook her head. "Not that I know of. Things have been tense between my ex-fiancé and myself but I don't think he'd go so far as to—" She broke off when Samantha started scribbling on the legal pad in front of her.

Samantha raised her head and shot Gabriel an icy glare. "I'm curious why you never suspected Mr. Letourneau. I mean, you did end up on his porch, after all."

Fate glanced at Gabriel. "Well—uh. That's funny. I don't why. I just *knew* he didn't do it."

"He's got an alibi anyway. Jason Turner said he discussed some business opportunities at length with Gabriel after the ball, during the time Fate was attacked," shot Niccolo in an irritated voice. "What's with that question, Sam? He's not even a suspect."

Samantha held up her hands, palms out. "I was just wondering. After all, Gabriel is pretty well wrapped up in this. Whoever did this was perhaps trying to strike at him through Fate. And as a Vampiric keeper, the list of his enemies is a long one."

It was true. He'd made many enemies over the years, and he'd begun ticking suspects off that list last night. Not many of the Vampir who wanted control of his territory would work this way, though. Procuring his territory was business and this was very, *very* personal. Drayden Lex was at the very top of his list of suspects because he was one Embraced who had a history of manipulating emotion to his advantage. Drayden was all about *personal*.

"So tell me again what you remember after your assailant bit your throat," said Samantha.

"It-it was almost like he hadn't meant to do it there in the street, but he just hadn't been able to resist. I felt his f-fangs rip through my skin and the draw of his mouth on my vein." She paused and drew a breath. "Then a curious pleasure came over me. I almost—*almost*—didn't care."

Niccolo had been leaning against the wall near Fate, listening. He stood and uncrossed his arms. "He used glamour on you. That's interesting."

Fate nodded. "I understand that he didn't have to use it. That it's optional."

Samantha shook her head. "And not logical. Why terrify you nearly to death only to have a change of heart and show mercy?"

Niccolo hummed in thought. "Maybe he suddenly grew a conscience?"

"Doubtful," Samantha shot at him. "Okay, what do you remember next?"

"He lifted me and brought me to his car," answered Fate. Samantha opened her mouth but Fate held up her hand. "Before you ask me the make and model, I don't remember. I don't even remember what color it was, or if it was an SUV or a sedan. Nothing. I was out of it by then, feeling drugged and fading in and out of consciousness. All I remember is watching the human stagger across the street and crawl into the front seat. He was cussing me out the whole time for kicking him the eye with the heel of my shoe, and for shooting him in the shoulder." She frowned. "By all rights, he should've been out cold. I *really* injured him. But I guess the glamour he was under was so powerful—"

"Humans can act like zombies when they're under the thrall of a powerful Embraced," Niccolo broke in. "They'll be half-dead and still be compelled to carry out the demands of the master who controls them."

Fate nodded. "I remember being thrown onto the back seat and the Vampir—" she drew in a sharp breath and let it out in a shudder " —climbed on top of me."

Gabriel's knuckles were white where he gripped the arms of the chair he sat in. He counted to ten slowly. Fate had gone silent. "Then what?" prompted Samantha.

"He forced my mouth open and I tasted blood." Her voice was shaking. "Lots of it."

"Do you think some of it spilled on the car seats?"

She nodded. "Uh—maybe. Probably."

Samantha jotted something down on the tablet in front of her. "Go on."

"Then—" Fate cleared her throat and her eyes grew bright. Niccolo grabbed a tissue from a box on the table with the coffeemaker and pastries and handed it to her. "Then—uh—" She made a small sound in her throat, fell silent and studied the tissue in her hand.

Gabriel stood. "*Fils de Pute!* Is this very necessary right now? Can't it wait until she's adjusted to the situation a little more and the wounds are not so fresh?"

"Gabriel, control your emotions," said Niccolo.

That was the problem; he didn't seem to be able to do that where Fate was concerned. Especially now, when she was hurting and he felt responsible for it.

Samantha shot him a chilly look. "This has to be done if we're going to find the perpetrators, Gabriel."

Fate shot up from her chair and paced to the table and back. "I'm fine! Just—just let me collect my thoughts." She paced back and forth a few more times, all the while tearing her tissue into little pieces. When she spoke next her voice was hard, forceful. Like she'd decided just to plunge through the whole thing to the end. "I drank his blood, and the strange part was I *liked* it."

"It was the glamour mischiefing your mind," commented Niccolo. "Making it easier for you."

She clenched the shredded tissue in her hand. "Right after that I went into—I don't know—some kind of heat. A sexual heat. I was repulsed by the thought of w-wanting my attacker that way, but it was so strong. I fought it tooth and nail, with every bit of my will…but I still—uh…" She gave her head a hard shake. "Anyway, the Vampir ignored me — ignored *it* — and crawled out of the back seat, climbed into the driver's seat and drove off."

"The human male was still with you?" asked Niccolo.

"Yes, he was sitting in the front holding his face and swearing a blue streak."

"And you never saw the Vampir's face? Not even when he was leaning over you, and was so close?" asked Samantha.

Fate stopped pacing, looked down at her shredded tissue and went silent. She pursed her lips and raised her eyes. "He never said a word. I never even heard him breathe. His face was painted black and covered with that huge hood. I didn't see him. I didn't hear him. I only felt him."

* * * * *

Fate rode silently the entire way home, staring out the passenger-side window. Samantha had revealed that while there hadn't been any prints found at the crime scene, they'd checked all the area hospitals and found a man who'd come in with a gunshot wound to the shoulder and a bad eye injury early that morning. Unfortunately, the man had been indigent and had given a false name. They were searching the area homeless shelters for him, but the lead was expected to be a dead end.

"So what's her deal?" she asked, ending the silence.

"Who, Samantha Ripley?"

"She seems to really hate the Embraced, yet... Well, let's just say that I don't think she's hating Niccolo very much. I was picking a lot of lust vibes in that department."

"Detective Ripley's mother was killed by a rogue Vampir when she was young. It's her mission now to see all the rogues caught or killed, and to be truthful she doesn't really like the non-rogue Vampir much better."

"But what about Niccolo?"

"Yes, she's very—uh—we'll say *fond* of him. She's worked very closely with Niccolo on a lot of cases."

"But Niccolo isn't *fond* back of Detective Ripley?"

"Not in the way she would like. Niccolo isn't one to develop relationships with women. Sex from time to time, *oui*, but never anything more. He must work with Detective Ripley, therefore hands off. No sex with her. Definitely nothing beyond that."

"I bet he doesn't have any trouble in the sex department. He probably has to beat the women off with a stick."

Gabriel laughed. "Yes, women flock to him. It has been that way for as long as I've known him."

"He has that darkly-handsome-brooding thing down to an art."

"Do you like the darkly-handsome-brooding thing?"

She turned her head to look at him for the first time. Sadness tinged her eyes even though she smiled. "I like whatever you are."

Chapter Five

Fate wrapped the blanket around her shoulders and curled her feet under her as she reclined on the couch in Gabriel's living room. She glanced at the phone and considered the ordeal of calling her aunt and her friends to let them know what had happened to her, but she just didn't feel ready for that yet. It would mean reliving the experience over and over. She grimaced. Maybe she'd feel more up to the task tomorrow.

Charlie—*Charles Alexander Scythchilde, but everyone calls me Charlie*—according to his introduction, wandered out of the kitchen and sank into a nearby chair.

Gabriel had left her with a couple Vampir he trusted while he attended to the business of running his territory. Fate believed he was really following up on her attack and simply hadn't wanted her to come along. Hence the babysitters—er—bodyguards.

The other one, Adam, was roaming the upstairs currently.

Her canvas stood in the center of the room. She'd fallen to her work soon after coming home from the police station the day before and hadn't stopped until this morning. She hadn't even slept. The intense concentration it took calmed her. Reliving the attack had been worse than the initial experience, and immersing herself in something as totally as she did with her painting helped to ease and divert her pain.

She squinted at the canvas and cocked her head to the side, studying it. She hadn't noticed it when she was doing it, but the man in the painting looked a whole lot like Gabriel. Same long midnight-colored hair, same gorgeous blue eyes. She frowned. What the hell was wrong with her? Lord, the man was beginning to consume every part of her. He was dangerous. She would have to get out of here soon, before she got her heart squished again. She did not want to schedule any more heart squishing on her calendar for a very long time—like eternity.

She turned to Charlie to distract herself from thoughts of Gabriel. How the hell did you make small talk with a Vampir? "So, Charlie, drink any good blood lately?"

Charlie smiled lazily and tipped his head to the side. "I think that's the first time I've ever been asked that question."

God, he was good-looking.

But *were* there any ugly Vampir? She hadn't seen any yet. It seemed a pity to call Charlie merely *handsome*. His face was so beautifully shaped that the description fell short. He possessed aristocratic good looks with his dark hair and eyes, and it was clear he had a very nice body under the tailor-made suits he wore.

And Adam was simply gorgeous. Adam had broad shoulders and a nice build. His hair was thick and blond and his eyes were a twinkling, mischievous blue. He had a square jaw with light five o'clock shadow and when he smiled, he had dimples. Fate was sure that women fell at his feet and likely Adam devoured each one with pleasure.

And Niccolo. He didn't even bear thinking about— light golden-brown skin, dark hair, dark eyes, broad shoulders and a body to slaver over. He had this way of looking at a woman that made them want to drop to their knees in front of him. His voice was like hot chocolate with a deep, seductive edge to it, and he had some accent that was hard to define. There was Italian at the heart, most likely. He swore in Italian from time to time, anyway. The accent, whatever its origin, was enough to curl her toes. The energy that rolled off him reminded her of a large, lazy lion at rest, yet the potential for power was definitely there. He was a very old one. She could feel it.

As gorgeous as they all were, however, they didn't hold a candle to Gabriel in her eyes.

"Oh, yes," said Charlie, answering her question. "I've had some intoxicating feedings lately. You?"

"One really good one so far." Fate shivered, remembering taking blood from Gabriel. Good lord, the man had affected her. She didn't think she'd ever been so attracted to anyone before. They needed to sleep with each other, and *soon*, in order to end this raging desire between them.

Oh, yes. Fate had an itch and its name was Gabriel. She needed to scratch it and get on with her bloodsucking life. She knew he likely felt the same. Gabriel had the look in his eye of a man who wouldn't be caged by one woman. That was fine with her; she didn't want to cage him. She just wanted him between her sheets once or twice.

"I can tell you're far from at ease with your new state of being," commented Charlie.

"Well, yes, I *was* raped of my humanity, after all."

Charlie leaned forward. "Hardly, Fate. You may no longer be human, but that doesn't mean you've lost your humanity. Humanity is a concept, a philosophical precept.

You'll have your humanity for as long as you choose to keep it."

She bit her lip. "I guess," she said finally. "I hear it's harder for the unmarked to adjust."

He sat back. "Yes. I was born with a caul, which means I was marked to become Vampir. Still, when I was Embraced, it was a little like your experience. It happened suddenly, although by accident, in my case. It was very jarring. But after it happened I adjusted quickly. It was like coming home, in a way."

She smiled and shook her head. "Not so for me. I feel like I'm in a foreign country and don't understand the language. But I'm good at accepting what *is* and can't be changed. I'm doing a lot of accepting right now." She shrugged. "Mostly because I don't have a choice. It's adjust or go insane. Those are my choices. Anyway, I learned a long time ago that bad shit happens to good people. It's how you deal with the bad shit that defines you as a person. You adjust, you grow stronger, and you hope that's the last of the truly bad stuff." She sighed.

Upstairs, the stereo blasted on, blaring Mozart's Requiem. Adam cursed loudly and there was silence. Two seconds later Nickleback poured from the speakers and stayed on.

Fate exchanged a look with Charlie and they both laughed.

"So how long have you known Gabriel?" she asked Charlie.

"Over a hundred years now, since I was first Embraced. He used to have territory to the east, New York City. Then Monia, my *mere de sang* — "

"Your blood mother? That means the one who Embraced you, right?"

"Yes. Monia and her mate Vaclav took it over and asked Gabriel to come here. There were problems in this territory before, but Gabriel cleaned them up."

"Why didn't you stay out east?"

Charlie shrugged and looked away. "There was someone out this way I wanted to be closer to."

She nodded, noting how his eyes had darkened before he'd glanced away. It had to be a woman he was referring to and, obviously, he didn't want to talk about it.

Adam walked downstairs and leaned against the archway that separated the living room and foyer, where the pocket doors were stored. He slanted a sexy grin at her. "Doing all right?" he asked.

While Charlie's voice and mannerisms were sophisticated, slightly bored and a little bit formal, Adam was relaxed and had a slight twang to his voice. Adam constantly seemed amused by something he alone was aware of. He possessed a boyish charm that made Fate want to smile.

Fate laughed. "I can't believe I have the best of Bostonian society from the Gilded Age sitting to my left and an honest-to-god cowboy on my right and you both drink blood to survive."

"The Embrace is the great equalizer." Adam made like he was tipping an imaginary Stetson at her and winked, "ma'am."

"Don't flirt, Adam," said Charlie. "I have a feeling Gabriel will have you by the throat again if you pull that with her."

He rubbed his neck. "Yeah, once was enough. I thought he was going pop my head off like a dandelion."

Fate glanced questioningly between the two men.

"Gabriel wrongly suspected Adam was your attacker and he went crazy," said Charlie.

"Oh, yeah." Adam nodded. "Insane."

"I've never known him to be like that," continued Charlie. "You're really under his skin, Fate. He's protective of you like I've never seen him. And over the years, we've seen a lot of tragedy, a lot of people who needed protection."

Rendered speechless, Fate couldn't respond. It pleased her deeply in a perplexing way to hear those words, and frightened her at the same time. Gabriel had the capacity to get into her heart and she didn't want him there. She'd let Christopher in and had given him everything, her trust and all her emotion, and he'd trampled on it all. He'd hurt her so deeply she doubted her capacity to ever be in another committed relationship. She'd had a couple one-night stands afterward, but they had been cold and empty. All about the sex and nothing more. Then her body had shut down and she stopped feeling sexual desire…until she'd met Gabriel.

Oh, yes, Gabriel had awakened her libido. And, lord, it had come to life with a vengeance. Fate had to make sure her heart was sufficiently armored against him to prevent any infiltration. She simply wasn't ready to have it broken again and Gabriel was obviously an accomplished heartbreaker.

But sex, that could be engaged in safely enough. That's all she wanted from a man now. And that's all they really wanted from her in the end, anyway.

* * * * *

Gabriel entered the darkened bedroom and spotted Fate's form curled up on the right side of his bed. She'd been choosing to sleep in *his* bed, though there were many other options in the house. Maybe she felt safer there. The moonlight slanted over her, silvering her face. She looked exhausted. Gabriel knew the trip to the police station had taken its toll.

The painting she'd done after she'd returned to his house was dark, angry. Done in deep reds and black, it showed a man and woman in a ferocious embrace. It could have been sexual or violent. The viewer could have a pick of the two and perhaps be correct either way. Gabriel had longed to touch her, simply to hold her. Instead, he'd let her work out her emotions in paint. After watching her for years, he knew she preferred the oblivion of work to tenderness that would make her lose her edge. He understood her well and respected that.

But now she was here. In his bed. Minus paint, minus canvas.

All his.

He pulled his shirt over his head and quickly lost his shoes, socks, pants, and boxers. He flipped the blankets back on the left side of the bed and slid in.

Gently, he took her in his arms. She wore a sexy light pink nightgown with silky, thin spaghetti straps. It was one he'd selected when he'd gone to her apartment. He knew it only reached her hips and was fastened together with a series of small, easily undone pink ribbons. Nearly transparent thong panties completed the scanty, revealing ensemble.

Gabriel's mouth went dry.

The material brushed along his bare skin as she murmured something unintelligible and rolled toward him. Her full breasts pressed against his chest and she shifted her leg, slipping it between his thighs as though it belonged there. She slid her arm across his stomach and snuggled in. Gabriel nuzzled her hair, smelling the hyacinth scent of her shampoo.

He wanted to roll her back into the pillows and drag his tongue over every inch of her body, lingering at his favorite places — the succulent flesh behind her knees, the place where her back met her sweet, curved bottom, and finally, but far, *far* from least, the smooth, tender spot where her inner thigh met her pussy. He'd move a few inches over from there and lick and lave in long strokes over her sex, delve his fingers within her to rasp over her G-spot, and lightly nip at her clit. He'd torment her until she keened for him, begged him to take her.

Gabriel shuddered at the thought, his cock hardening.

Fate sighed in her sleep and brushed her fingers over his chest. He studied her face. Dark circles marred the creamy skin beneath her eyes. She slept the deep healing sleep of the newly Embraced. As much as he wanted to awaken her, have his way with her, he couldn't be so selfish. He'd take her soon enough and it'd be all the more sweet for the wait.

Gabriel closed his eyes, content just to be near her, while he reviewed the failures of the day. He'd checked out Christopher Connor and his girlfriend, Lisa. He'd wondered if perhaps one or both of them could be connected to what had befallen Fate. Perhaps Lisa was trying to get back at Fate out of jealousy? Unfortunately, Gabriel had discovered nothing except the fact that Connor was now cheating on Lisa with another woman.

The police had not yet returned results on the blood samples. Perhaps that would lead to something useful. Although, even if they were able to correctly identify and locate the indigent human man who'd jumped Fate, it was most likely the Vampir who'd utilized him had used glamour to erase his memory of the incident. The human would probably tell them nothing but a story of how he'd awoken on the street somewhere with horrific wounds of unknown origin.

Gabriel pulled Fate closer to him and set up the mental field around the house so he would know if anyone came within. No matter how long it took, he'd find Fate's attacker, and at any cost he'd ensure she stayed safe while he did it.

* * * * *

Fate opened her eyes and blinked, orienting herself to Gabriel's still unfamiliar bedroom. She rose from the bed without needing to flip back the covers and realized instantly she'd awoken to the realm of dream.

There were several different levels of this place and she recognized that she was in the lower level, the one right above waking reality. This was where she often encountered the dark, malevolent creatures she now understood were the Dominion. A low, rhythmic tone, a sound she often heard while she dreamwalked, filled her awareness.

She glanced at the bed and saw Gabriel lying there, holding the sleeping Fate in his arms. It was such a domestic scene, such a touching sight. She stood for long moments, studying Gabriel's handsome face, which was lighted by the silvery moon's illumination. He looked content to have her in his arms.

The tones grew louder; a signal she intuitively knew meant she needed to move because the Dominion were nearby. She turned and walked out of the bedroom and down the hallway.

Gabriel's house was virtually the same in the realm of dream as it was in waking reality, though the shadows were different here. Seemingly alive, they writhed and moved, nipping playfully at her heels with velvet teeth and moving out of her way when she walked so she could see ahead of her. The shadows were always her friends when she traveled through this place.

She walked down the stairs and into the living room. Adam was asleep on the couch, one long arm thrown over the armrest and a blanket tangled between his legs. Charlie was nowhere to be seen.

The tones increased in tempo and volume, and Fate went on alert. That was a signal that enemies were nearby – the dark ones, the ones who lived in this world that was just parallel to waking reality and fed from those who were unaware while they dreamed. They were vampires of a different sort.

The Dominion.

Fate glimpsed a flash of light from the corner of her eye and whirled. There, in front of her, was an ethereal, gaunt form.

"Ahn-nyong," he greeted her in Korean. He bowed.

Suddenly, she felt like she was back in the dojang. Glancing down, she realized she still wore her nightgown. With a thought, she changed into stretchy black pants and a tight black shirt that she could fight in. She clad her feet in heavy boots that would hurt when they connected in a kick, and she pulled her hair up into a ponytail with another thought.

Fate bowed, then stood in battle stance in front of the Dominion warrior.

"Why so combative, Fate?" the creature asked. "I have done nothing to indicate I want to fight you."

"We always fight. Why should tonight be an exception?"

"Because tonight we don't want to play with you, or test you." He paused for a heartbeat. "We just want to kill you."

"You can't kill me in this place. You don't have that kind of power."

The beast laughed. "You're so young, Fate. You have so much to learn. I feel privileged to aid in your education." He bowed again.

Light flashed all around her, and she was surrounded by Dominion. Her heart started to pound in her chest, and her muscles tensed in anticipation of battle.

One of them stepped forward and she rushed him. He blocked her hit with his inner arm and she spun around, bringing her elbow solidly into his solar plexus. The breath whooshed out of the thing and she brought her arm up just in time to land a back-fist strike to his face. She turned and finished him off with a right reverse punch. The thing screamed and disappeared in a burst of light.

What did that mean? Had she killed it? Or had it simply retreated and moved to different part of the dream realm?

Two more of them approached her and she attacked fast and hard. She landed a middle section punch to the first one's abdomen, then brought her leg up and spun to the left in a roundhouse kick that caught the second one in the face.

More of them closed in around her, but she was faster and stronger than they were. She moved with lightning speed, in a blur of movement, picking each one off easily. One by one, they disappeared.

With a flash, the last one disappeared and she stood alone in the living room. All was quiet. Beyond the walls, the crickets chirped. Adam gave a loud snore from the couch and turned over.

Fate relaxed from her battle stance. She had a lingering sense of the Dominion, like an energy pattern imprinted within her. She wondered if she could track a Dominion using it. Following her hunch, she closed her eyes and concentrated on it. With a whoosh of motion she was familiar with, she felt herself transported. She opened her eyes and found herself standing next to a bed. A Dominion hovered over the prone figure of an adolescent girl. Light coursed from the girl to the beast.

Fate reached out, grasped the creature's leg and yanked. "Get away from her," she yelled.

The Dominion disengaged, looked around and snarled. It floated to its feet and immediately attacked. She blocked its blow, whirled to the left, came up behind it and struck, knocking it to the ground. It reached around, grabbed her by the ankle and felled her to her back on the floor. Her breath didn't whoosh out of her lungs here, as it would have in waking reality, but she still felt the impact. The thing pinned her down and wrapped paper-dry, reptilian-like hands around her throat.

Fate gasped for breath and concentrated, pushing upward with her will rather than her muscles. Both she and the Dominion shot upward. The Dominion slammed against the ceiling, squealed angrily and let her loose. When they floated to the floor, Fate whipped her leg around as hard as she could, nailing the thing in the face with the heel of her boot. It screamed and disappeared.

"Fate, wake up."

She felt someone shake her physical body that still lay back in Gabriel's bed.

"Fate?"

She opened her eyes and gasped. Drawing huge gulps of air, she sat up. When she coughed, Gabriel rubbed her back and murmured to her. Finally, she calmed and swallowed hard. Waking up had been akin to pulling a fish from water. She noted somewhere on the edge of her awareness that the gray light of dawn now stole around the curtains on the windows. Morning. "Amazing," she rasped. "It's never been like that."

"The Dominion?" asked Gabriel.

She closed her eyes and nodded. "They wanted to kill me. I mean, usually, *always*, we battle. But this—this was like nothing I've ever seen before. They were very, *very* serious this time."

"Yes."

"I see what you mean, Gabriel, about me being a special threat. I must be because..." She shook her head in disbelief. "But I was stronger, faster and could fight better. I could feel their energy and use it to track them over distances. I had more control and I understood the tones this time. Before, I never did."

"The tones? I have never heard tones before."

"Yes. There are tones in the background when I dreamwalk. I never knew what they were before, but this time I understood that they're a type of communication." She went silent and bit her bottom lip. "From somewhere."

"Are you all right?"

She turned and smiled at him. "I beat them. They almost killed me before I did, but I still defeated them. I destroyed them. Well, I think I destroyed them, anyway. But they said something that confused me. Gabriel, can they kill me over there?"

"Unfortunately, yes. They've always had the ability to take your life, Fate. But now that you're Vampir, it will be very difficult for them."

"They said they could, but I don't understand how. It's the realm of dream. It's not real, it's all illusory."

"It is real, Fate. It just runs by a different set of rules. That's how the universe works. Just as we can end their existence, they can end ours. But, as I said, it's extremely difficult for them to kill any Embraced, let alone one with abilities like yours."

She slipped out of bed, suddenly energized. "All I know is that it was incredible. I feel great now. I feel—"

He leaned toward her. "Like you have a purpose?"

"Yes." She did a little dance, twirling in her nightgown and wigging her bottom in celebration. "I can battle the Dominion in the realm of dream. It felt so good to move and fight. Over there I wasn't exhausted all the time from being newly Embraced."

He smiled. "You have found your calling, perhaps."

"Maybe so. It felt *right*."

Smiling, Fate stopped in the middle of the room and regarded Gabriel. Her mouth went dry. He was looking her up and down like he was a starving man and she was breakfast in bed.

Gabriel leveled his dark gaze at her. His eyes were hooded, his body tense. Sexual intention radiated from him, warming Fate, flooding her pussy. Everything Gabriel wanted to do to her seemed to be in his eyes at that moment. As though, right this very minute, he was deciding just how he should consume her from a million possibilities. As if he contemplated in just which manner he would take her.

Fate shivered in anticipation.

"Come here," he said in an aroused, low rumble.

She walked toward him, barely realizing she did it, and stood next to the bed.

He rolled off of it and stood with a powerful, lazy grace that reminded her of a large cat.

He leaned in and nipped her earlobe. "And I want to lap up your cream," he growled softly.

She sucked in a breath. "Can you hear my thoughts?"

"You haven't learned to block them yet, Fate, so yes, I can hear the loud ones." He circled, sauntering in a predatory manner, examining her from head to toe. His body heat caressed and warmed her skin as he moved closer. "And that was a loud one."

He stopped in front of her, slipped a finger under the one of the spaghetti straps and rubbed her skin. The hungry look on his face made her breath catch. Holding her gaze, he dropped his hand down and undid one of the small pink ribbons binding the top of the lacy nightgown.

Fate's breath came faster. "What am I thinking now?" she asked in a voice that sounded throaty and aroused to her own ears.

Gabriel chuckled and then growled low. "I can concentrate on nothing but your luscious body when it's so close to this bed." He undid another ribbon. Now her breasts were all but exposed. The material hung precariously on each taut nipple. One slight move and it would fall.

He stared down at the curve of her breasts. "There is no reason for us not to consummate what this is between us right now. We are all alone. Adam is downstairs on the couch, but in this room, it's just you and me, Fate."

"And the bed," she murmured.

He untied the last ribbon and Fate moved her arms, allowing the top of her nightie to drop to the floor. She stood in front of him, clad only in her sheer panties. He looked her up and down, a smile curving his sensual lips. "And the bed," he purred in agreement.

Fate reached out and grasped the long, wide length of his cock in her hand. He was gorgeous beyond description, rock-hard, and huge. She worked him against her palm and he tipped his head back and groaned. God, she wanted him so badly. Wanted him in her mouth, and then in her body.

Still holding his cock in her hand, she stepped forward and kissed his chest. He twined his fingers into her hair as she began her descent down his hard, glorious body, kissing every available part of him she could until she rested on her knees in front of his shaft.

She kissed the head of him, drawing a deep groan from his throat. "I want to finish what we started before," she murmured and then licked him.

The bedroom door slammed open, revealing Adam who wore a horrified expression on his face. "Gabe, you gotta come now. I mean *now*."

Silence reigned for a heartbeat. Adam's face slackened as he took in the scene he'd barged in on.

"That's what I'm *trying* to do," Gabriel ground out.

"Me too," Fate said on a sigh. She covered her breasts with her arms, stood, and backed away. Again she'd been doused with cold water just as she'd been ready to rid herself of this unreasonable attraction.

"God, I'm sorry. I wouldn't interrupt unless it was really important," said Adam. "And this is."

Gabriel let out a string of curses. He stalked across the room and pulled both his and her bathrobes off the hook on the bathroom door. "This better be for something *really* serious, Adam."

Adam paled at the audible note of violence in Gabriel's voice. He nodded. "It is, swear it. Never saw anything like it in my life and that's saying a lot."

Chapter Six

Gabriel stalked to Fate and put the bathrobe over her shoulders. She stood, securing it around her. Her pussy almost hurt, she was so aroused. To have been so close to finally assuaging her need for Gabriel and then to have it so abruptly curtailed was the worst kind of torture.

Barefoot and bathrobed, they followed Adam down the hallway and descended the stairs. It was early morning and while pale gray light filtered in from outside, the house was still dark. At the bottom of the stairs, Fate reached to flick a light switch. Adam moved with vampire speed and took her wrist to stop her.

"No," he said. "Bad idea. Stay away from the windows and doors." She dropped her hand and looked at the front door. A long piece of stained glass decorated it. Beyond it, she could see forms out there, moving around.

Gabriel went to a window and carefully peeked out. "*Mon dieu,*" he groaned. "News of Fate's attack must've leaked. The press is all over my front lawn."

"They're everywhere, Gabe," answered Adam as he peered out the window. "Front yard, side yards, backyard. I disconnected the phone, but Niccolo let me know telepathically that they're over at Raven House, too."

Fate sank down onto the stairs. So much for calling and breaking the news to her friends and her aunt herself. They'd find out on the local news. Acute regret pinched her.

Gabriel headed for the front door.

"Boss, what are you doing?" asked Adam.

"I'm going to tell them to go away. They cannot be here. I've set up a mental barrier around the house for Fate's safety. They will confuse it if they wander too close to the structure."

"You're in your bathrobe, Gabriel," Fate pointed out. "Anyway, they *want* to know we're here. That's the whole reason they're camping out. If you go out there, it'll only make them more determined to stake out and wait for us to leave the house so they can barrage us."

"Gabe, she's right," said Adam. "Let me go out. I'll convince them you're not here. That might buy you some time."

Gabriel stopped in the middle of the foyer with his back to them. "Yes, fine. You're probably right." He turned. "Do that, Adam, and then call Niccolo and Charlie over here. Mihail flew in from Texas last night where he's been keeping an eye on Drayden. Tell him come over here, too. I want a lot of muscle around to protect Fate while we decide the best course of action."

"Right. You all go on upstairs." Adam made a shooing gesture. "Uh—go back to what you were doing. It'll calm you down." He shot a meaningful look at Fate. "Calm is good. Let me handle this. Consider me the ultimate protector of your privacy from here on out as payment for my interruption."

With a heavy sigh, Fate stood and headed back up the stairs. Gabriel followed her. Mood broken, she went into an upstairs sitting room where she'd seen a television set earlier and flicked it on. Taking the remote, she sank into the chair in front of the set and flipped through the channels until she saw a picture of herself—not a very good one, either, goddamn it—on one of the local morning news programs. She upped the volume.

…Harding, one of Newville's most successful artists and one who has earned the devout patronage of celebrated businessman and financier Dorian Cross was attacked early Sunday morning. In a rare and disturbing act, the vampiric assailant Embraced Miss Harding against her will…

She flipped the set off. She'd seen enough. A cold, hard ball settled into her stomach. "God," she whispered at the black television screen.

"I'm sorry, Fate." She looked up to see Gabriel standing in the doorway. "I had hoped it wouldn't leak, but these kinds of stories, anything regarding the Embraced, are highly sought after. It's why we try to keep such a low profile."

She could only sigh at him in response.

"We may need to leave the city," he continued. "I have friends, Aidan and Penelope, who live about an hour and a half from here, out in the country. They have a horse farm. I was thinking we could go stay with them. It's very peaceful out there."

"No." She shook her head. "No, goddamn it. I'm not going to leave my life here. I won't let this asshole, whoever he is, or the press run me off."

"Admirable sentiment," answered Gabriel in a voice backed by steel. "But we will do what we must to keep you safe." His tone brooked no disagreement. "I will not allow you to be endangered." He reached into his bathrobe pocket, pulled out his cell phone and tossed it to her. "Call who you must, Fate. There are people who are likely very worried about you."

She caught the phone. "Thanks," she said, but when she looked up, he was gone.

Fate spent the next two and half hours on the phone with her aunt, friends and a few close business associates. She couldn't contact Dorian, though she spoke to his secretary, Cynthia, who told her he was in meetings all morning. Was she all right? Did she need anything? Where was she? Cynthia fired off questions and asked for all the juicy details. Loath to reveal her location to *anyone*—not even her closest friends, and definitely not to Dorian's assistant—Fate simply said she'd try him back later that day.

By the time she was done, a sensation had begun curling and clenching in her body. It was a feeling like she'd never experienced. Instinctively, she knew it was the *sacyr*. She was a young Vampir and she needed to feed. Blood called to her now. Stubbornly, she tried to ignore it, though it was really too intense for that. She set the cell phone down on a nearby table and headed into Gabriel's bedroom to dress.

She had a life to lead, goddamn it. Embraced or not. And she was going to lead it. Sometime today she had to get out of this house and back to work. She had galleries to visit and accounts to settle.

She went to the window and carefully pulled the curtain just a little bit to the side. The reporters were starting to trickle away. Apparently, Adam had been convincing. At least that was good news.

The sound of shower spray came from the bathroom. Hmmm...Gabriel naked in the shower. There were definite possibilities there. Fate let the curtain fall back into place, closed *and locked* Gabriel's bedroom door and then padded into the bathroom.

Her jaw had dropped the first time she'd seen his bathroom. It was enormous. Three sinks dominated one wall — why someone would need three sinks in their master bathroom was a mystery to her — and a huge whirlpool bathtub large enough for at least four stood in the corner. A series of white wicker cabinets and shelves lined the wall and a door leading to a large walk-in closet stood on the opposite end of the room. Plush white carpeting covered most of the floor.

The focal point of the bathroom was the shower. It stood in the center of the room encased in frosted glass. It was almost a room unto itself — large enough for several people. Many water jets shot from various strategic locations, making the shower feel more like a full-body massage.

Gabriel was nothing if not hedonistic.

She could see him in there in now, under the hot spray of the water. Fate turned, closed the bathroom door and locked that one, too. The world could be coming apart and she wouldn't care. She just didn't want any more interruptions.

Fate undid her robe as she walked toward the shower. Her bare feet sunk into the plush carpeting with every step. The silk of her robe slithered down her body to the floor. She opened the shower door and stepped inside. The whole place was filled with so much steam she couldn't even see Gabriel. A jolt of uncertainty rocketed through her — was she even sure it was *Gabriel* who was in here? The way their luck had been running, it probably wasn't.

"It's me," came Gabriel's voice near her ear. His arms enveloped her and his chest pressed against her back. He dipped his head and brushed his lips across the nape of her neck. She felt his breath stir the small hairs there. At the same time, he closed his hands around her waist and molded her body to his. His skin was warm and wet. "I'm so happy you decided to join me, *ma cheri*," he murmured into her ear.

She turned to face him. His eyes were dark and intense—as dark and intense as the *sacyr* and sexual heat that had unfurled within her own body. Neither was riding her easy right now. It wasn't being easy on Gabriel either, judging by the expression of concentration on his face.

He twined a hand to the nape of her neck, the other to the small of her back, and pulled her up on her tiptoes to meet his mouth. The length of her body pressed flush up against his, and every breath or slight movement rubbed her nipples into stiff little peaks. She ran her hands up his biceps, over his shoulders, and attacked his mouth with every bit of passion she had in her. They ate at each other's mouths, licking, sucking and nipping—like they couldn't get enough of the taste of each other.

They weren't directly in the hot stream of the showerheads, but the spray of it had thoroughly wet her. Their bodies slid against each other—warm and slippery. He broke the kiss and worked his way down her throat to her nipples. He sucked on one while he plumped and caressed the other breast with his free hand. She felt his lips working over her hardened nipple and the gentle scrape of his teeth over it. She practically wept between her legs. Her whole sex seemed to throb from the want of him.

He trailed his tongue over her skin to the other nipple and attacked that one, too. Fate tipped her head back and twined her fingers through his hair. "Gabriel, yes."

He trailed his hand down to part her thighs. Softly, he brushed his fingers over her labia and drew a lazy circle around her clit. Pleasure shot through her pussy and she thrust her hips forward, wanting more.

Gabriel licked his way down over her stomach and through the hair of her mound. Then he went to his knees, pressed his palms to her buttocks and pulled her pussy to his face. She felt his tongue flick out to lap up her juices and tease her clit in long, persistent licks.

Her knees went weak. She gasped and grabbed his shoulders to prevent herself from toppling over. He supported her by cupping her bottom, holding her with her thighs spread so he could feast on her sex. His tongue played leisurely with her pussy lips, driving her insane. Finally, he found her entrance and pushed inside. With agonizing slowness, he fucked her with his tongue.

It was too much.

"Gabriel," she moaned.

He lowered her to the smooth, wet floor of the shower. Her back arched as he spread her thighs as far as they could go and held them there. He lowered his mouth to her once more and licked up her sex from her anus to her clit in long, mind-numbing strokes. Then, in an unhurried manner, he nibbled and sucked at her pussy lips, moving up to her clit.

She tossed her head back and forth. "Please," she pleaded with him. "Fuck me, Gabriel. I need you."

Blessedly, she felt him shift and the head of his shaft press against her. She moved her hips against him and he grabbed her wrists, pinning them to the floor on either side of her. "You want me within you, love?" he asked.

It was the only thing in the world she wanted right now—Gabriel Letourneau fucking her senseless. She wanted this desire for him sated. "Yes, please, I'm going crazy."

With one long, hard thrust, he impaled her. Her vaginal muscles had never been stretched so far before. She'd never been so filled by a man. The sensation was indescribably good. She let out a long, shuddering sigh of relief. That's what she needed.

Gabriel closed his eyes. "Ah, *ma cheri*. You feel so good. So hot, so sweet. I don't know if I can be gentle with you this time."

She shook her head. "Not gentle," she managed to get out. "Just fuck me."

He instantly pulled back and impaled her again, then set to shafting her hard and fast. It was what she wanted and needed...and it pushed her over the edge right away. He released her wrists and she grabbed onto his arms as she climaxed hard.

He didn't falter, but kept up the pace of his thrusts—the thick, ridged length of him pistoning in and out of her. He held her by her waist, and his hips hit her inner thighs with every inward stroke, making a slapping sound of flesh on flesh.

She couldn't think. She could only feel his skin rubbing against hers, the soft spray of the water and the in and out slide of his cock. Her breath came faster as her second climax built inexorably.

Without withdrawing, only slowing his thrusts, he gently took her left leg and shifted it over so it touched her right. In this position, she lay on her side. Then he helped her to her knees, so she was once again on all fours and he was taking her from behind.

She lowered her head to her forearms, pressed her bottom up and spread her legs. The tiles were hard beneath her knees, but she barely noticed it. He resumed his hard and fast pace, drawing loud moans from her. This position made the penetration deeper and every thrust rubbed the head of his cock over her G-spot.

He moved his hand down and slid his finger over her wet clit. His finger slipped back and forth over it easily. The teasing way he touched her almost drove her insane. He'd bring her close to orgasm, then slow the pace of his caress, keeping her on the edge and building an extra strong climax. In this position, with her thighs spread and him behind her, her clit felt exposed and vulnerable to him — and, God, how that turned her on. Gently, he teased it back and forth, rubbing over it and circling it as he thrust his cock into her.

Another climax took her hard and fast. She felt her vaginal muscles clench and release around his shaft as she came. He kept stroking her clit afterward — gentling her straight into another orgasm. She almost screamed with the intensity of the next one.

This time he came too. He thrust deep within her and she felt his cock pulse as released himself into her.

"Oh, yes," she hissed.

He pulled out of her and gathered her against him, scattering kisses over her forehead and face. "Your body was made for mine, Fate," Gabriel murmured. "Your blood was made to flow in my veins and mine in yours."

What he said scrabbled at the edges of her awareness, making her uneasy, but the word *blood* overshadowed it all. The *sacyr* roared within her. Her fangs lengthened. She moved to straddle him, but fast as lightning, he rolled her beneath him. His eyes were dark—but this time not with sexual lust. This was about feeding.

"We can satisfy each other in all ways, love," he said. "Take from me what I take from you." He parted his lips and she glimpsed his lengthened fangs.

She arched her throat in offering and he took it. His fangs brushed over her skin in a caress and his tongue stole out to lick her skin. Then, without warning, he bit. Sweet, sharp pain infused her body, followed quickly by indescribable bliss. She'd been afraid the bad memories from her attack would rise up and turn Gabriel's bite into something nightmarish, but it was a sexual dream instead.

She grasped his arms and arched her spine, pressing herself more fully against him. His hands slipped around her, cradling her against him as he drew on her life force. She parted her thighs and he slid between them easily. He found her pussy and pushed within her. She closed her eyes and sighed in pleasure.

Take from me what I take from you, came Gabriel's voice in her head. She started in surprise. She knew telepathy was a part of being an Embraced, but that was the first time she'd experienced it directly.

She lowered her mouth to the place where his shoulder met his neck and licked. It was wet from the shower and tasted salty. In that moment, the *sacyr* twisted in her stomach and she could it take it no longer. She bit and felt the sweet give of his skin. With a little *tick* within her mind, she unfurled her glamour for the first time and covered him. She knew it wasn't as powerful or smooth as his, but she did her best to make it pleasurable for him.

She wove the glamour from pure instinct. Refining would come later.

His blood filled her mouth. She closed her eyes, feeling it flow through her veins, nourishing all the neglected parts of her, giving her strength. His cock slowly glided in and out of her at the same time, and they seemed one single animal, joined by sex and blood. It was an intimate experience, intimate beyond all her imaginings.

Gabriel released her throat and threw his head back on a groan. "Ah, Fate," he rasped. He increased the speed and angle of his thrusts, pressing her buttocks and the small of her back down against the tiled floor of the shower. Her next climax came fast. She released his throat and cried out as they both came together.

He wrapped her in his arms and rocked her back and forth as they enjoyed the rush of the blood through their veins and the afterglow of their joining.

* * * * *

Fate Embraced

That was the headline of the newspaper that Adam put on the table in front of Fate that afternoon. "Isn't that clever," she commented with a sour twist to her mouth. "Like I haven't been enduring puns on my name since I was five." She picked up her coffee and took a sip as she read through the article.

She'd come downstairs after showering with Gabriel—and they really *had* showered, eventually—to find the house filled with Embraced. Adam, of course, was still there. Charlie had returned with Niccolo and they'd brought a friend.

Mihail was a fully Embraced who had an intriguing Slavic-sounding accent she couldn't place. She was too afraid to ask him where he was from because the man was even more intimidating than Niccolo. He'd spent a full five minutes sitting on the couch with a scowl on his face and staring at her with an ice-blue gaze that gave her chills. The man was just disturbing. Finally, she'd turned her back on him and started reading the newspaper.

Hot, consuming wisps of anger curled through her by the time she reached the end of the article. They'd spotlighted her life, her family, her personal history, her art—everything that made her who she was. They'd done it without asking her permission and had laid her open for all to see. It was as if, like her attacker, they'd stolen a piece of her.

She wanted some semblance of her life back, which meant not cowering in Gabriel's house. She needed to reclaim normalcy. Well, as normal as she could get on a steady diet of hot blood.

In order to regain normalcy, she needed to find out who'd attacked her. She needed closure. She'd tried to get Gabriel to let her to go with him when he investigated the various leads he had, but he never allowed it. He said she was not strong enough yet to defend herself if it came down to that.

She hated that he was probably right, since she *was* tired all the time.

Although it still pissed her off that he thought she wouldn't be able to handle herself if it came to that. She was a black belt in Tae Kwon Do, goddamn it! That hadn't changed when she'd become Vampir. It made her angry to feel so vulnerable. After all, she'd spent years studying Tae Kwon Do simply so she would never feel exposed and defenseless. Now all she seemed to feel was exposed and vulnerable.

She tossed the newspaper to the side and chewed her lower lip. God, she was frustrated on so many different levels! Sick of waiting. Sick of being cooped in the house while Gabriel fought her battles for her. Sick of having her life on hold. Sick of feeling like a victim.

Fate looked up and watched Gabriel as he talked with Charlie. He'd dressed in all black, as he so often did. The dark cable-knit sweater he wore draped nicely over his wide shoulders and across his powerful chest. He'd twisted his long hair into a knot at the nape of his neck. The length was still damp. She hoped that episode in the shower had rid of her system of him, but looking at him now — and instantly wanting him — made her realize that was not the case…yet.

He turned and looked at her. Everything that they'd done in the shower seemed to be in his eyes. She flushed, not with embarrassment, but with instant carnal hunger.

Remember what I said, said Gabriel telepathically. *Your body was made for mine, Fate. Your blood was made to flow in my veins and mine in yours.*

Fate froze like a deer in headlights and then looked away. She didn't want that kind of sentiment from him. She wanted his body, naked against her, and his cock, hard and moving within her. She didn't want his emotion, or empty promises. Most of all, she didn't want to be hurt again — duped and cheated on like with Christopher. Instinctively, she shut her mind to him — threw up walls a mile high.

He'd been watching her for five years and knew her well. That was all fine. She'd known him only a couple days and not under the best of circumstances. How could he be throwing words like that at her already? She didn't want words like that *at all* from him.

Ever.

Fate stood. "Charlie, do you have a car here?"

Charlie turned to her with a question in his eyes. "Yes," he said carefully.

"I need to get out of here, go check my accounts at a few galleries around town. Can you give me a ride?"

Gabriel stepped forward. "Fate, I don't think leaving right now is the best idea."

She shrugged at him. "The reporters are gone. Adam diverted them for the time being. I see no reason why I can't get back to business as usual."

"It's not safe for you to be out there and exposed," said Gabriel, his voice hardening. "I called Charlie, Niccolo, and Mihail *here* to help protect you from whatever malevolent force has chosen to target you."

She shrugged again. "So the muscle comes with me." Fate turned and walked toward the front door.

Strong hands grasped her shoulders and turned her. Storm clouds enveloped Gabriel's face. She drew a sharp breath at the darkness in his eyes. "I will not allow anyone to harm you, Fate, but you are making my job more difficult," he said.

"Why do you even care what happens to me, Gabriel? It's not like we're in a relationship. It's not like there are real feelings involved here. Why are you going to so much trouble over me? If it's because I ended up on your porch and you feel responsible for what happened—don't. Shit happens—every day and all the time, especially in my life. I don't hold you responsible, so you shouldn't either."

Gabriel stood staring at her for a long moment. Confusion replaced the storm clouds on his face. Ah—and there it was. Even he didn't know why the hell he cared what happened to her. He released her and turned away. "Go with her," he ordered toward the general vicinity of the other Vampir. "I have to see to something of vital importance."

Without a backward glance, Fate grabbed her purse and coat and headed out to stand on the lawn. Tears pricked her eyes, but she didn't understand why. She'd wanted to remind Gabriel they were just convenient bed buddies, nothing more, and she'd done it.

So why the hell did she feel so bad? Like she just got sucker punched? She was growing dangerously attached to a man who would ultimately hurt her.

She was in free fall.

Niccolo headed up the bunch of Vampir that exited behind her. They piled into Charlie's Jaguar. She rode shotgun and Mihail—who still hadn't uttered a word— and Niccolo climbed in back. She told Charlie where to head and they pulled out into the street.

Heavy cloud cover hid the sun. She was thankful for that. Not that being Vampir precluded her ability to go out into the sun. It just wasn't preferred. Whatever chemical changes that had taken place in her body made her hypersensitive to the sunlight. It seemed brighter and hotter now than it had before she'd been Embraced and that made her want to avoid it, generally. But Gabriel was brighter and hotter than the sun today, it seemed, and avoiding him was far more a priority.

She looked over her shoulder and saw Mihail scowling at her. She scowled back, then glanced at Niccolo and jerked her head toward Mihail. "What's with the silent sucker?"

"I can speak," said Mihail.

"Okay. So why don't you do it more often?" she asked him.

"I have nothing to say. I don't speak just to hear my own voice."

Well. Couldn't really argue with that logic, could she? "Where are you from, Mihail?"

"New York."

She laughed. "I meant *originally*. You still have a hell of an accent, Mihail, and it's not from Brooklyn."

"Recently from New York, originally from the area around Prague. I am new to the United States and have spent most of my life living in the region I was born in. That is why my accent is still heavy."

Wow. That was the most she'd heard him say since she'd met him.

"Mihail is a very old friend of Monia and Vaclav's. You've heard us speak of them, haven't you?" said Charlie.

She nodded. "Monia is Gabriel's *mere de sang* and Vaclav is her mate. They took over the New York City territory."

"Yes," answered Niccolo. "Mihail and Vaclav are some of the older fully Embraced. Can you feel the power he gives off?"

"Yes. I can feel it from you, too, Niccolo."

"I am old, Fate. I was born in 54 A.D.," said Niccolo.

Charlie cleared his throat. "Mihail was born in 264 B.C."

"Oh, my God," she breathed.

"Yes," answered Charlie. "That's what I said." He pulled the car over to the curb in front of the Eastside Gallery. "Here we are." He shut off the engine.

She glanced through the glass window on the front of the gallery and caught a glimpse of a familiar, silver-haired man. Dorian was in there. "Uh—you guys can stay here, okay? I won't be long and nothing in there will hurt me, I swear."

"I really think—" started Niccolo.

She quelled him with a look. "It will attract far more attention if I go in there with three muscle-bound, very conspicuous, eye-candyish Vampir flanking me than it will for me to slip in there, settle my account, and slip out—no fuss, no muss."

Niccolo glowered at her and said nothing. His lack of acquiescence shone bright and clear in his chocolate brown eyes, however. He opened his car door. "I promised Gabriel I wouldn't let you out of my sight. We're coming in, Fate." Charlie and Mihail also got out of the car.

She sighed. "Okaaay, fine," she said to the now empty car. Fate got out, slammed the car door shut and let them tail her into the gallery.

The Eastside Gallery was decorated in muted colors, mostly shades of gray—colors bland enough not to take away from the artwork on display, yet classic and elegant. Dorian had been able to get her in here, as he'd been able to get her in everywhere. She owed a lot to him. Fate frowned as she noticed that the paintings of hers that had been displayed up front just a couple weeks ago were now absent.

"Fate," crowed Dorian from across the room. He hurried across the floor toward her wearing a concerned expression on his face. When he reached her, he took her hands in his. "I heard what happened. Are you all right?" He eyed her bodyguards with obvious trepidation.

"Who hasn't heard, Dorian?" She smiled. "All things considered, I'm very well."

"So, is it true? Are you—are you one of *them*, now?"

She sighed and nodded. "Yes. Unavoidably and unalterably...yes."

He did something then that chilled her blood—*he pulled his hands from hers.* "I'm so sorry, Fate," he said in a low voice, the kind reserved for condolences at a funeral home.

"Hey," said Charlie beside her. "It's not like she contracted a communicable disease."

Dorian looked up at him sharply and turned into the man she barely knew—the cold, hard, arrogant businessman. "Isn't it? Who are you, anyway?" he asked with no small amount of undisguised scorn.

Niccolo flashed his extended fangs. Apparently Dorian had pissed him off enough to trigger them. "Her bodyguards," he growled.

Dorian stared at him with the look on his face that likely many an executive had suffered over a boardroom table. It wouldn't make any of her current company tremble, however. "More *Vampir*," he sneered.

"We know who you are, Dorian," Charlie broke in. He flicked a glance of regret at Fate before continuing. "We know about your support for a certain bill making its way through Congress right now. We know about the money you're spending in support of it."

Dorian stared hard at Charlie and gave him a tight smile. "Is that some kind of a threat?"

Charlie smiled back. "Not at all. I'm just stating the facts."

Dorian's smile faded. "Call me later, Fate. We'll talk *privately*," he said without looking at her, and walked out the door.

She stared after him, swallowing hard. Bills? Congress? Support? *What?* Not to mention that Dorian's behavior had just thrown into relief how different her life would be from now on. As an Embraced, she would be a pariah to many humans. Dorian included, it seemed.

Mihail came to stand beside her. His strong, smooth energy rolled off him and enveloped her in a velvety sense of protection. "They either love us or they hate us," he said, seeming to read her mind — and maybe he had. "There are no neutral feelings from their kind to ours. It has always been so, and shall always be."

A strong hand cupped her shoulder. "Go. Do what you came here for," said Niccolo.

She shook herself out of her trance and went to find Simone, the manager of the gallery. Surprisingly — or perhaps not — all of her paintings had sold. That had been why none of them had been hanging in the gallery's lobby when she'd entered. The publicity had made her paintings a hot commodity. Of course, her sales had nothing to do with people actually *liking* her work. The fact she was a fully Embraced had brought her instant fame and fortune.

Simone was *all about* wanting more of her paintings, of course. How soon could she drop them by?

Charlie drove her to the other two galleries in town that carried her paintings. It was the same story at each.

Fate had just come into a sizeable amount of money, and if she acted fast she could make much more.

Funny that she wasn't happy about that.

She collapsed into the passenger seat after the last stop. The sun had already sunk in the sky and the stars were out. "Oh, God," she said with a heavy, tired sigh. "Charlie, take us back to Gabriel's."

Charlie gave a sharp shake of his head. "Not Gabriel's, Raven House."

"What?"

"Gabriel contacted me to say there are a couple reporters on the lawn at his place and to bring you to Raven House for the night."

"Oh." She opened her mouth to ask if Gabriel would meet her there and then snapped it shut. Fine. If he wanted to shuffle her off for the evening, she'd shuffle. It'd be even better if she could shuffle off home, but everyone would probably throw a serious fit if she tried to do that. Man, it was tempting, though. She *so* wanted to be between her own walls, in her own space.

On the drive across town, Fate's thoughts turned back to Dorian. His behavior with her made her think that perhaps he was on the radical hating side of the Embraced issue. She'd never before considered his views on the matter, and the subject had simply never come up in conversation. She'd considered Dorian enlightened and educated, but perhaps he wasn't.

"Charlie, what did you mean when you told Dorian you knew he was supporting a certain bill through Congress? What certain bill?" Fate was tuned into politics and had protested against a few of the pieces of dangerous legislation that had threatened the Embraced. Following the Embraced "issue" was a hobby of hers. Her psi abilities made her different from others and therefore she'd always felt a kind of kinship with the Embraced.

"Are you sure you want to know?"

She cringed. She hoped he didn't say the Hartham and Cooper bill that would form a federal agency to "watch" the actions of the Embraced and give agents free license to "rein in" any of those activities they deemed dangerous. Basically, it gave the agency the ability to kill any Embraced, any time, for any reason. "Yes," she squeaked.

"The Hartham and Cooper bill."

Damn.

"He's been gaining the support of certain politicians who are on the fence over the issue by promising to help them get reelected by basing his businesses in their cities and giving sizable campaign contributions. Basically, he's throwing his money around."

She shivered. "There can't possibly be enough support for that bill." She gave her head a hard shake. "It won't pass."

Charlie shrugged. "Dorian is doing his part to make sure it does. We don't know if he'll succeed yet, but we're watching the whole situation very closely."

"I never knew," she said quietly.

"I'm making inferences here, but I'd make a guess that he keeps his beliefs private." His lips twisted in a wry smile. "You don't seem like the type to withhold, so you probably weren't as secretive. He probably understood you two would contrast sharply on the subject, so he chose to avoid it."

"Perhaps."

"Humans are like sheep, Fate, and we are the wolves—their predators. They understand that. It is primal and instinctive to want to guard against us. Our very existence strikes at the heart of their fear of death."

"Yes, I understand that."

She stayed quiet for the rest of the drive across town, contemplating her confused feelings. Finally they pulled up to the curb in front of Raven House. It was, *surprise*, also an old home. This one was Victorian, with a large wraparound porch. Like Gabriel's home, it was enormous. She walked through the front door into a large living room. Many people were arranged on expensive-looking pieces of antique furniture, talking and laughing. It reminded her of a posh dinner-party, except instead of smoked salmon as an entrée it would be something...*else*. Something red. Every last one of them went quiet and still, watching her with curiosity. There was a very faint fizzling sound in her eardrums and she thought maybe she was registering the large presence of Demi in some extrasensory way.

Charlie walked in behind her. "Everyone, this is Fate. She'll be staying here tonight. Please make her feel welcome."

A beautiful blonde dressed in a long, slinky gold dress separated herself from the group and sauntered toward her. Sex was in every single sway of her nicely curved hips. She walked toward Charlie, but kept her gaze trained on Fate. Fate watched her warily, not liking the look in her seemingly innocent blue eyes.

The woman threaded her arm around Charlie's waist, laid her head to his chest and coyly traced a line over one of his nipples through his shirt. Charlie shuddered. Fate suspected from pleasure. "She smells like Gabriel," the woman commented.

Fate frowned. She did?

"Yes," said Charlie with a tired sigh. "She does."

"She's the one Gabriel has had at his house, isn't that right?" she asked, eyeing her speculatively. "She's the one he watched all those years."

Annoyance flared within Fate. She thrust her hand out. "Hi, nice to meet you. Didn't catch your name. Oh, and by the way, I'm standing *right here*." She shot the woman a beaming smile. Would she catch the sarcasm or was she too ditzy?

Frowning, the blonde lifted her head from Charlie's chest. "Charlie," she said in childlike consternation.

"Fate, meet Laila," said Charlie. "Laila, Fate."

Laila pulled away from Charlie. The full pout of her lower lip trembled. "Gabriel has marked this woman with his scent!" She turned and fled up the stairs, crying. Charlie shot her an apologetic look and pounded up the stairs after her.

"Okay," she muttered. Great, now she felt like a real heel. She hadn't been here three minutes and she'd already made someone cry.

Something soft brushed her leg. She looked down and saw a large brown and gold tabby cat. It was Niccolo's familiar, Kara, most likely. Gabriel had told her about the cat. Fate knelt and drew the animal into her arms. Kara was large, soft and comforting. Fate pressed her nose into the cat's fur and closed her eyes. God...it was all too much.

"Laila fancies herself in love with Gabriel," said Niccolo somewhere above her. "And Gabriel will have no part of her anymore because of it. He's afraid she'll grow too attached to him. *Dio*, she already is."

Fate sighed. "I just want to go to sleep," she mumbled into Kara's fur as she clutched the cat harder. Patiently, Kara allowed it. Soon Niccolo walked away.

When she'd collected herself, she gave the poor cat her freedom, stood, and spotted Charlie's car keys on the table beside the door. She bit her lower lip. It really wouldn't be nice of her to steal Charlie's car, would it? But she longed for her own apartment. For home and for things that were familiar surrounding her. Her own four walls. Her own things. *Normalcy*. Even if it was only a temporary illusion.

She could have that just for one night, couldn't she? She glanced around. It appeared that Charlie, Niccolo and Mihail had gone to bed. She could go home just for a few hours and get back before dawn. They'd never even know she'd been gone.

Decision made, she snatched the keys and was out the door.

Chapter Seven

"I have told you repeatedly. I'm not the man for you, Laila." Gabriel reached out to touch one of Laila's heaving shoulders, but pulled back. It would be cruel to send mixed signals, even if he only meant to comfort her.

"You-you don't know what it's like, Gabriel," she sobbed into her hands. She raised her head and stared at him with lovely, tearful eyes. "To love someone with everything you are and not have it returned. It happened with Xavier," she whispered raggedly. "And now you." She pushed up from the couch where they sat and raced out the door.

When Gabriel had walked through the door of Raven House, Laila had confronted him about Fate as if Laila was a lover scorned. Gabriel had decided then to sit down and have a serious discussion with her. It wasn't the first of such discussions between them, but this time his words seemed to penetrate. Maybe it was because he'd talked of Fate in terms of deep caring. That was the first time in as long as he could remember he'd ever talked of a woman in that way. It had made an impression on Laila, as well as on himself.

Fate lay upstairs now, sleeping. The newly Embraced needed much rest and he'd worn her out last night.

Charlie sat nearby. He shot up from his chair as if to follow Laila, but Gabriel raised his hand. "Let her go. She needs time alone to think."

Charlie speared Gabriel with an icy stare. "Easy for you to say, you don't care about how Laila feels. You don't *know* how she feels. *I do*." Charlie stalked toward the door.

Yes, he did. Gabriel sighed. Charlie had come from one of the best Boston families in the late 1800s. He'd been born with not only a caul—marking him as destined to one day be Embraced—but also a deformity that marred his handsome face. Unable to look at him, his father had tossed him out as soon as he could, forcing Charlie to survive on his own for many years. When Monia, Gabriel's *mere de sang*, had Embraced Charlie, the deformity had disappeared. However, the blow to Charlie's heart, dealt by his family, had never healed.

That hurt had been compounded by his unrequited love for an Embraced named Penelope and his subsequent loss of her to Aidan, her current mate. All of that had occurred well over a hundred years ago. Still, Gabriel knew Charlie had yet to fully resolve the issues. Now he seemed to be enamored with Laila. That, too, seemed ill-fated.

Charlie paused by the table in the entryway and turned to him. "Where are my car keys? I put them right here." He looked out the door. "Where is my *car*?"

"Fate," Gabriel muttered as the possibility of her flight suddenly loomed in his mind. He shot from the couch and took the stairs two a time. He checked the available bedrooms and didn't find her.

Adam appeared at the opposite end of the hallway. "What's wrong, Gabe?"

"Did you see Fate tonight?"

He shook his head. "But I heard what had happened when she got here."

Gabriel forcibly controlled his emotions. Heart-stopping images of all the horrible things that could have already befallen Fate flashed through his mind. He would *not* let anything happen to her. He forced calm into his voice. "What happened, Adam?"

Adam held up a hand, palm out, as though to hold him off. Maybe he wasn't doing such a good job at feigning calmness after all. "I wasn't here, Gabe. I don't know the whole story. All I know is, according to Niccolo, she had a hard day and was upset before she arrived here at the house. Then Laila had a tantrum at her over you."

Gabriel took a measured breath. "Okay, fine," he said with forced composure. "That helps explains things. I think she took Charlie's car and left. Tell Niccolo and the others I'll let them know what's going on, all right? I think I might know where she went." He turned and walked out the front door of Raven House. Gabriel stood for a moment on the porch, closed his eyes and shifted. His body became lighter, freer feeling. With a couple strong flaps of his wings, he was airborne. He could move faster in raven form.

Gabriel flew straight to Fate's apartment and spotted Charlie's car outside immediately. He alighted outside her door and transformed back. The negative part of shapeshifting was that it left him naked at his destination, but, as an older Vampir, he could produce the illusion of clothing.

He pulled the shadows toward him, cloaking himself in the velvetiness of them, and produced an illusion of black boots, jeans and a dark-colored sweater. Using telekinesis, he opened the lock on the door and entered.

All the lights were off in her apartment, though a few candles provided soft, flickering illumination. Incense scented the air along with jasmine bubble bath. Fate, dressed in a long nightshirt, lay curled in the center of her bed, blankets tangled around her legs, her hair — still damp from bathing — spread out over the pillows. She slept deeply, unconcerned, content to be in her own bed, in her own home. Although her Glock lay on the bedside table beside her, letting him know she wasn't taking any chances.

He watched her sleep, as he had so many times before, but this time it was different. His feelings for her were deeper and more complex. He'd spent the whole day thinking about the woman who lay on the bed before him now and had realized how much he cared for her, how much he wanted to keep her in his life.

Maybe he'd felt this way about Fate for longer than he cared to think about. On some level, maybe he'd begun to feel it during all those years he watched her. After all, even though she had not directly been a part of his life, he'd let himself get closer to her than he'd been to anyone in a very long time. He'd shared her happiness and her disappointments. He'd suffered through the criticism of her artwork, and her nasty breakup with Christopher Connor. During that time, he'd linked himself with her unknowingly and, little by little, he'd come to see the beauty and vulnerability in her soul. Maybe he'd even grown to love her at some point back then, but had just consciously realized it recently.

Gabriel believed Fate might come to feel for him the way he felt for her, but fear had a chokehold on her. Not only did she have an entirely new existence to adjust to — which was more than enough on its own — but less than a year ago she'd been devastated by Christopher Connor. She'd truly believed he'd loved her and she'd given him a large part of herself, only to be deceived and hurt in the end. It made sense she was cautious now. She didn't trust him not to hurt her. She wouldn't trust *any* man not to hurt her.

Gabriel lowered himself onto the bed beside her and rubbed a tendril of her hair between his fingers. *So silky. So soft.* Fate made a small noise in her throat and rolled onto her back. God, she was beautiful. But that didn't change the fact that he was *irate* that she'd endangered herself the way she had this night.

He leaned over and quietly opened a drawer by her bed, pulled out two of her chiffon scarves and gently tied her wrists to the bedposts. She was a deep sleeper and Gabriel could move with preternatural stealth when he chose. His cock hardened from just the act of securing her to the bed and leaving her open to his every sexual whim.

He returned to his place beside her and stroked his hand down the side of her face. "Wake up," he whispered.

She inhaled sharply and opened her eyes. "Gabriel," she breathed. She tried to move her arms and discovered her predicament. "What are you doing?" she asked.

"Do you trust me, *ma cheri?*"

She struggled against her bonds. "Gabriel, let me go!"

He cupped her chin and directed her gaze to his. "Do you trust me, Fate?" he asked again. "Do you believe I'd ever do anything to hurt you?"

She went still. Her lips parted as she stared up at him. "Uh—I trust you...physically. I don't think you'd ever harm me physically."

That was a carefully worded answer. He ran his finger over her lips. The words that went unspoken were loud and clear, *but not emotionally.* "That's a start, I guess."

"Will you let me go now?"

"Fate, what if you'd awoken and it hadn't been me you'd found hovering over your delectably—" he raked his gaze down the length of her "—vulnerable body right now?"

He reached down and cupped her breast through the long silk shirt she wore for pajamas. Her nipple peaked against his palm, and her breathing hitched and then let out in a long sigh. "What if you'd awoken to find someone who meant you harm, instead of pleasure?" he asked as he leisurely teased her hardened nipple. "There would have been no one here to come to your aid."

"Okay, you made your point," she said, her voice trembling. "I know it was irresponsible of me to do what I did tonight. I just needed to be home. I needed a little normalcy and familiarity. I freaked, all right? After all I've been through, a little bit of freaking should be understandable."

He eased his hand down the plump of her breast, over her stomach, and let it come to a rest on her waist. "Maybe. Except this little episode of freaking could have gotten you killed, and that would not have been understandable at all." He stared into her eyes and put all his emotion into his gaze. "I don't want to see you hurt. Do you understand? Seeing you harmed would kill me."

She blinked twice and swallowed hard. Her eyes were wide and sheened with unshed tears. "A woman at Raven House said she could smell you on me. She said you'd m-marked me," her voice shook. "What does that mean?"

"Laila said that, didn't she?"

She nodded.

"You're too young yet to have developed an acute sense of smell. One ability of the Embraced is the capability to scent another on someone if they've been close, say, rubbing up against each other—" he raised an eyebrow " —or were making love together on the shower floor."

Her brows drew together. "Why do you call it making love?"

He went silent. It had been *making love* to him that morning. Deep down he believed she didn't consider him just a fuck, either. It went deeper than that. He just had to show her. "I don't know when it happened exactly, Fate, but sometime during all of this I fell in love with you."

"Let me free, Gabriel," she said. The tears in her eyes were gone. Sharp anger replaced the sorrow he'd seen in her only a minute earlier.

"If I let you free, you'll run."

"Damn right. I'll—"

"Hush. I can smell you now," he interrupted her. "And know you're excited by this. By being tied up, unable to stop me from doing anything I want to you. I know this is one of the fantasies you hold so silently within you."

She bit her full bottom lip, and then let it go in an unconscious gesture of contemplation. Gabriel couldn't stop himself from leaning over and sucking it into his mouth. She let out a small moan. He closed his eyes, enjoying the feel of her soft lip between his teeth.

He'd been in her subconscious mind and knew this was one of her fantasies, to be tied up by a man, and he was more than willing to be the man. He loved having her bound and at his mercy. That way she couldn't run away from him.

"You enjoy being vulnerable to me," he murmured against her mouth. "I can do anything I desire to your sweet body now, and you can't do a thing to stop me."

"Gabriel," she whispered. "Why do you affect me this way?"

He smiled. "I'm glad you can admit I affect you at all. Now admit this is a fantasy of yours. Admit what I already know, that you're aroused right now."

He pulled back to watch her face. Her eyelids were heavy and her lower lip was plumped and rosy from his attention. She ran her tongue over it and he watched with rapt attention. "Maybe," she answered in a throaty voice.

Maybe? He gave a short laugh. Right now, she was every bit as aroused as he was.

He dropped the illusion of clothing and straddled her legs. Her eyes widened at his erect cock. Gabriel unbuttoned the first button of her nightshirt and brushed his knuckles along her satiny skin. "I think it's past time I showed you just how much you're mine."

Her eyes flashed angrily. "I'm not *yours*, Gabriel. We're in this for a good time, nothing more. We've been thrown together by some shitty circumstances and we're making the best of it. There's no possession involved here—no emotion. I'm nothing you can claim. When this is all over, I'm walking away and you'll be happy I did. Happy you got what you wanted from me and can move on to the next woman."

He flicked open the next button, revealing more of her flesh. "You confuse me with your ex-fiancé, Fate, and you lie to yourself. I intend to show you just how much."

She opened her mouth to shoot back a retort, most likely. But he undid another button and slipped his hand inside her shirt to cup her breast. Fate snapped her mouth shut as he plumped it and drew his fingers softly back and forth over the erect nipple.

"Mine, Fate," he purred. "I want you to be mine. I want you to desire to be mine."

He kept one hand on her breast and undid the rest of the buttons with his other hand. The silk of her shirt whispered over her skin as he parted it. He ran both his hands down her body to her thighs. Her lush, pretty pink pussy was exposed to his view, glistening with the liquid of her excitement. Her full breasts were tipped with hard little red nipples and her chest rose and fell with her increased rate of breathing.

He drew his hands over her shoulders feather light, hearing the rapid pitter-patter of her heart. Caught up in the silken smoothness of her skin, he trailed them down over her breasts and stomach, down the length of her legs and then back up again. His fingers grazed her sex as he went. He wanted to touch her there, but first he wanted to memorize every hill and valley of the rest of her.

"God, you're beautiful," he murmured as he continued to worship her with his hands. His gaze ate her up from head to toe. "How will I torment you, Fate? Oh, there are so many ways." He slipped his hand to her pussy and caressed her.

* * * * *

Fate's entire reality narrowed to his hands on her. Every inch of her skin felt sensitized from his attention. He slid two fingers within her, stretching her muscles, and brushed his thumb over her clit. She arched her spine and moaned his name. He'd secured her hands and made her entirely helpless, and *damn*, did it turn her on.

He moved up her body, rubbing his glorious cock over one of her breasts and then across her lips. She wanted so much to taste him. On the second pass of his cock over her lips, she snaked out her tongue and licked the head of his erection. Her lips closed over the head of his shaft, making Gabriel shudder in pleasure. He thrust his hips gently, pushing his length into her mouth. She sucked on him greedily, licking up the pre-come from the slit in the head of his cock. He moved his hips back and forth, thrusting gently into her mouth. She closed her eyes and reveled in the taste of him.

"Fate, your mouth is so sweet," Gabriel said through gritted teeth. "You're killing me." He pulled his cock away from her. "Any more and I'll come."

She opened her eyes. "Would that be so bad?"

He lowered his mouth to her breast and fell to the task of sucking and licking her nipple. "I want to come in you," he said around a mouthful of flesh.

"The night is young. We can do it all."

Gabriel moved away from her breast and kissed her throat. She arched her neck in a gesture of submission and felt the hard brush of his fangs along her skin. She thought for a moment he'd bite her—oh, how she wanted to feel the mark of his mouth on her—but instead his tongue touched the skin just under her ear. She moaned at the sensation of the hot tip of it running over her collarbones and then lower, down between her breasts, over her stomach.

"Gabriel," Fate pleaded breathlessly. She was so wet for him, so ready.

He drew his tongue down her skin with agonizing slowness, dipping it into her belly button. He continued lower, over her pelvis and down to her inner thigh. There, he kissed the crease where her leg and pelvis met.

Fate's clit was aroused and infused with blood. It pulsed with the desire to be caressed and licked. He ran his tongue along her skin, leaving tiny, hot kisses along the way...headed straight for her pussy. He licked her labia and then—blessedly!—twirled his tongue around her clit.

She arched her spine at the sensation and pulled on her bonds. "Oh, yes," she moaned.

He groaned low in his throat. "You taste so good. I would never grow tired of your flavor, Fate."

She stiffened at his words, but he licked her from anus to clit with big, lazy swipes of his skillful tongue and she forgot what had upset her. She writhed at the feel of his hot, slick tongue exploring her sex. He pushed it inside her and fucked her with it, drawing a low moan from her throat.

Gabriel slipped a finger within her and then a second while he laved her clit. Slowly, he massaged the inner walls of her pussy with his fingers while he continued the torment with his tongue. He added his teeth to the mix and lightly nibbled at her clit. When her body tensed for climax, he pulled away.

"Gabriel?" she gasped in question.

He said nothing. He came back and built her up again, only to pull away once more.

Fate thought she'd go insane. "Gabriel!" she said, panting and pulling at her bonds. "You're going to pay for this."

He gave her long tongue swipes, lazy as a lion bathing himself in the sun. "Consider this punishment for the worry you put me through tonight, *ma cheri*."

"And I've been properly punished, Gabriel," she cried. "Please, *please* fuck me now."

"Mmmm. Your pussy is plumped and flushed with arousal. Your nipples are standing at attention. Your body cries out for my cock within you. But when I enter you, Fate, it will not be *fucking*. What is developing between us goes further than the base, primal demands of our bodies. Don't you agree?"

Good god, she'd agree to anything right now, the devious bastard! She twisted as much as her restraints would allow. Her sex throbbed with need. "Okay, sure!" she cried.

Gabriel gave a low laugh. He moved to her bedside table and removed something from her bottom drawer. "That did not sound very convincing." He held up her dildo. "Let's see how else I can tease you."

She looked at him and narrowed her eyes. "You're evil."

"I think you like me when I'm evil." He dropped the dildo on the bed beside her and returned to the business of tormenting her. He traced his fingertips down slowly over her stomach and pussy and circled her anus. "No man has ever taken you here before, has he, sweet Fate?" he purred as he teased the tight ring of nerves.

"No," she said breathlessly. His finger was already slick with her juices and he breached the entrance easily. "Oh," she moaned at the feeling of all those nerve endings being stimulated. He thrust, widening her.

"Mmm, you're so tight there," he murmured. He leaned over her body and brushed his lips against her breast. As he slowly thrust his finger in and out of her anus, he sucked and licked on her erect nipple like it was a piece of hard candy.

Fate grabbed onto the silk scarves binding her wrists and closed her eyes. He was going to drive her insane with pleasure. Surely, that had to be his goal.

He pulled out of her body, reached over and took a tube of lubricant from her bedside drawer. After he squeezed out some of the lubricant, he pressed two of his thick fingers to the tight ring of muscles and thrust. She gasped as his digits slid in and out of her. Her muscles gripped his fingers tight. He continued for long minutes, relaxing and stretching her muscles, exciting her to the point of uncontrollable moaning and squirming — likely preparing her body to take the toy.

"You would like to experiment wouldn't you, *ma cheri*?" he purred. "You do want to feel my cock...*everywhere*, right?"

She couldn't answer, couldn't even think. She felt his fingers pull free and the slick, soft-gelled head of her dildo press against her nether opening. He pushed it into her slowly, inch-by-inch. It wasn't nearly as wide as Gabriel's cock. Still, it seemed large enough to stretch her to a place where pleasure and pain combined in one overwhelmingly erotic sensation. She whimpered and rotated her hips, wanting more.

"Tight," he growled. "You're so damn tight." He thrust it in with little movements, until she was completely filled. After waiting only a heartbeat, he started pulling it out and pushing back in repeatedly, fucking her with it. It excited all those little nerves she hadn't even known were there and made her writhe in pleasure. Soon she keened with the need to climax. She wanted something within her pussy. Something to ease the empty ache she had inside her. She'd never been so turned on in her life. God, she felt combustible.

"Please, Gabriel. Please," she begged.

He ignored her plea, but she could see the strain of this on him. His face was flushed, his jaw clenched. His eyes were dark and hooded with arousal. She needed to breach his ironclad resolve. "Imagine how my pussy will feel—so hot, tight, and warm. I'll hold you so close, Gabriel...so close. My muscles will ripple and pulse around your cock. Imagine it."

"Witch," he growled and Fate suspected she'd succeeded in breaking his control. Gabriel left the toy thrust up within her and draped her legs over his shoulders.

"Yes," breathed Fate as he positioned the head of his cock at her entrance.

"Tell me there's more here than lust, Fate," Gabriel said through a clenched jaw. His fangs were extended and his eyes looked black, they were so dark. "Tell me there's a possibility between us. Admit to at least that much."

Confusion swirled through her. She did care about Gabriel, very much. So much it frightened the absolute hell out of her. Especially since she'd only known him for just a few days. She had to regulate those feelings, though. She couldn't let herself get hurt again. Nor could she completely deny them.

"I-I admit to a possibility," she whispered.

With a roar, he thrust into her. He slid in and seated himself to the hilt. The combination of the toy filling her anus and Gabriel's larger member filling her pussy snapped her head back in a rush of satisfaction. An instantaneous climax overwhelmed her. She clenched the scarves in her hands and screamed as it shattered over her.

Gabriel set up a punishing rhythm, pistoning hard in and out of her. He sent her an image of how they would look to someone watching them. She saw the muscles of his finely shaped ass flex as he sank into her pussy over and over between her spread thighs. She saw herself, tied to the bed, arms above her head, completely at the mercy of the man who fucked her.

He shifted his hips a fraction of an inch to the side, changing the angle of his thrust. He slammed into her again and again, growling as he shafted her, and she came again. Colors she hadn't even known existed exploded before her eyes as her second climax engulfed her body. As she'd promised, the muscles of her vagina pulsed and clenched around his shaft. He threw his head back and came with a low groan.

He came down on top of her and undid the ties around her wrists. She wrapped her arms around him. He kissed her deep, exploring her mouth with his tongue.

"Ah, *ma cheri*," he murmured against her lips. "You slay me every time." His cock twitched deep with her, still hard. "One time I'd like to make love to you slowly, instead of in this fervor."

She smiled against his mouth. "Trust me, I don't mind the fervor."

He rocked his hips back and forth, thrusting into her with agonizing deliberateness. Her breath caught. The toy still filled her anus and the dual sensations were indescribably erotic. She closed her eyes and sighed.

Gabriel rotated his hips and increased the speed of his thrusts. He lifted up, grabbed her waist and held her as his pace grew faster and harder.

Fate tossed her head back and forth as another climax crested within her. He shifted, driving into her with long, hard strokes. Her orgasm broke over her in a blinding wave, robbing her of all thought.

He pulled himself free and urged her to her stomach. Then he pulled her hips up, so her buttocks were offered to him. He pulled the toy from her body...and thrust his cock within to take its place. Gabriel was wider than the dildo and stretched her even more exquisitely. He shafted her gently at first, then harder and faster. Gasping, Fate fisted the blankets and held on for dear life as another climax built.

Gabriel reached around and stroked her clit as he plunged into her, sending Fate to the edge of another orgasm. Finally, he groaned out his second climax and took Fate with him.

Breathing heavily, they collapsed in a tangle on the bed. Gabriel pulled her to him and brushed the hair from her face. Her muscles were weak and she felt barely able to move in the aftermath of her climaxes. She fell into an exhausted sleep as he scattered kisses over her forehead. The last thought she had before she drifted off was of *possibilities*.

Chapter Eight

Fate adjusted the water streaming into Gabriel's bathtub and tested it with her finger. Finding it perfect, she untied her bathrobe and sat on the edge of the tub to wait out the fill. The sound of the rushing water lulled her as the steam clouded the room.

Her thoughts drifted back to the night before last, when Gabriel had tied her to the bed. She shivered at the memory in spite of the rising heat within the bathroom. God, the man knew just what buttons to push, and he'd dialed up heaven on her body that night.

Even if some of the things he'd said had bothered her.

She'd managed to avoid him the next day and he'd been away last night and all of today consulting with SPAVA and investigating a lead he had with Niccolo and Charlie. One he wouldn't share with her, the bastard. These days he was paying special attention to a few rival Vampir on the Council of the Embraced, ones that had a reason to see Gabriel suffer and may have used her as a pawn to achieve that goal.

He'd left bodyguards with her, of course. Adam and a few other Vamps she'd never met before. She'd stayed away from them, mostly, and had used the time to lose herself to her painting. Perhaps as a way to *not* deal with the jumble of confusing thoughts that seemed to rule her mind these days.

It seemed she couldn't escape them now, however.

She sat on at the edge of the tub and drew her fingertips through the water, remembering an anniversary she'd shared with Christopher. He'd rented an expensive hotel room with a huge tub like this one. There had been chilled champagne waiting and a delicious catered dinner. Fate had believed then that she'd never been happier. Christopher had made her feel as though she was the center of his universe. She'd felt so safe and loved with him.

Cherished.

About six months later, she'd found a receipt in the back pocket of his pants while she was doing the laundry. A little investigating had earned her some disturbing information. He'd taken Lisa to that same hotel. That's how Fate had discovered Christopher had been cheating on her. He probably would have continued right up to the altar and beyond if Fate hadn't broken it off with him.

She reached over and turned off the faucets. Gabriel also made her safe and, yes, even loved. He made her feel cherished, and, oh, she wanted to feel cherished by him. But how could she open herself up to him so quickly? She chewed her lower lip and grasped her robe to push it from her shoulders. Trusting Gabriel was such a risk. One that—on top of all the other drastic changes in her life, recently—she wasn't sure she was ready to take.

"Hello, Fate."

With a gasp of heart-stopping panic at the unfamiliar masculine voice, she grabbed her Glock, jumped up, whirled around, and aimed. A tall man with dark brown hair, chiseled features and snapping green eyes leaned against the sink.

She had a line of sight trained straight at his head, but he didn't even flinch, goddamn it. Instead, his gaze traveled slowly down her body and back up. She glanced down, realizing her robe had fallen open and closed it with a snap, still keeping the gun trained on her target.

He pouted a little and let his gaze settle on her face.

"*Who* the *hell* are you?" she demanded in a voice so angry it shook.

"Hello, Fate," he repeated. "How strange that sounds. How poetic. Fate…naked and holding a gun on me."

Fate's body went taut as a bowstring. She was a new Vampir, a baby Vamp, essentially. Would she be strong enough to fight this much older Embraced if she had to? Fear-tinged scenarios flicked through her mind. She pushed them away, knowing she needed to stay cool and calm.

She cocked her hip and sighed. "Yeah, whatever. Go ahead, quip on my name. I'm used to it." She feigned a yawn with one hand, still keeping the Glock trained on him. "And your name is?"

He flashed a set of white teeth that uneasily reminded her of a wolf. "Drayden Lex."

Oh, *shit*. Gabriel had told her all about this guy. Not someone she wanted in the bathroom with her. *Calm*, she reminded herself. She raised an eyebrow. "*Drayden?* Oh, like your name is better. I bet you really got teased in school."

He laughed. "I like you." He shook his head, the smile fading. "And I won't hurt you. Do you realize how quickly I could disarm you, anyway? You can put the gun down, Fate."

"Uhm, I think I feel better with it up, if you don't mind." She kept it trained on him. "Look, do I need to scream for the *five* Vampir downstairs now?"

He shook his head. "I mean you no harm. I'm merely paging your lover, Fate. Gabriel now knows I'm here and is rushing to your rescue." He spread his hands. "I need to talk to him." His full mouth curved in a smile. "I figured popping in on the beautiful one that shares his bed would bring him racing."

"What the hell does threatening me have to do with the fact you need to talk to Gabriel?"

He flashed another smile. "*Everything.*"

About two heartbeats after that, Gabriel arrived. He wore all black—midnight-colored boots, jeans and sweater. His hair was long and lost in the darkness of his clothing. Fate couldn't tell where his sweater ended and his hair began. His eyes were dark too...full of dangerous storm clouds. If she hadn't already been backed up to the edge of the bathtub, she would've retreated.

Gabriel extended his hand at the same time he said, "What the hell are you doing here, Drayden?" Drayden went flying backward into the mirror behind him, shattering it.

Drayden landed hard on the bathroom counter and rolled off, lithe as a cat, to stand on the floor. He chuckled as he brushed the mirror shards from his clothing. "Is that any way to treat a houseguest, Gabriel? What happened to your sense of hospitality?"

Are you all right, Fate? he asked telepathically. *Did the bastard hurt you?*

I'm fine, she answered. Adam and the other vamps had shown up and now hovered outside in Gabriel's bedroom, right behind him.

Drayden held up his hands. "I didn't come here to fight, Gabriel. Do you really think I'd just pop in here alone if I had any nefarious plans in play?" He laughed. "I'm not suicidal. I know you could kick my ass easily on the home court."

"You *always* have nefarious plans in play, Drayden," Gabriel answered. "It only makes me more suspicious when you say you don't."

Drayden laughed and wiped his cheek, where blood from a shallow cut welled. He turned toward Fate and said conspiratorially, "He still has his panties in a bunch from that whole thing in Paris in 1721." He waggled his eyebrows and licked the blood from his hand.

She crossed her arms over her chest. "You mean that time you murdered that baker and his whole family?"

Drayden blinked innocently. "Uh—my fang slipped?"

She rolled her eyes.

Drayden turned to regard Gabriel. "Man, you really got it bad, huh? You're telling this one everything. What happened to your policy of fuck 'em and leave 'em?"

"Why the hell are you in my territory, Drayden?" asked Gabriel.

He gave Fate an appraising look. "I had to see the woman you've been breaking everybody's balls over." He nodded. "Nice, Gabe. Real nice. She's a beauty. I can see why you've been all over the region lately, interrogating every Vampir that crossed you or merely looked at you wrong in the past 350 plus years, and generally pissing everyone off."

A muscle in Gabriel's jaw worked and his eyes flashed dangerously. "Why—"

Drayden held up a hand. "Before you go giving yourself another seven years bad luck, I only came to tell you something." He shrugged. "Well, okay, and to yank your chain a little bit just because it's fun. Look, here it is. I didn't attack her, so call off your dog, Mihail."

Silence descended. "I'm just supposed to believe you?" Gabriel asked finally.

"Look, I have other things going on right now, man. Other irons in the fire. I don't have time to mess with you or your territory at the moment. That doesn't mean I won't in the future, but right now I'm not." He spread his hands. "I'm being honest here, Gabriel. It's a rarity. Take it for the gift it is."

Gabriel merely stared at him.

Drayden glanced at Fate and back at Gabriel. "Because of the personal nature of the attack, I'd say it's someone close to one of you. Real close. All I know is, it wasn't me. I came here *alone* to prove I mean no harm to you and yours, Gabriel. All I want in return for my candidness is Mihail out of my territory, out of my *face*. Got it?"

A tense silence descended. Fate thought the two men looked like circling wolves with their hackles raised.

"If you leave without incident, I will consider what you've said, and I may, or may not, pull Mihail," Gabriel said finally.

Drayden stared at him. "I think if you ponder long and hard you'll figure out I'm telling the truth. Figure it out fast, Gabriel. Mihail is breaking my balls."

Gabriel smiled. "I'm sure Mihail is enjoying every minute of it, too."

"I don't have time to *entertain* Mihail at the moment and he's getting in my way."

Gabriel flashed his fangs. "Get out of here, Dray. You are unwelcome in my territory."

Drayden smiled slowly, and then glanced at Fate. "Bye, beautiful. Don't worry, if you hang around with this one for a while, you'll see me again." He winked, then transformed into a huge white owl and flew out door, making Gabriel's men scatter.

Adam stepped inside the bathroom. "Did the bastard touch you, Fate?"

"No. We exchanged a few choice words and then you all showed up."

"He knew it'd be a goad to Gabriel coming in here and sneaking up on you like that," said Adam.

"Drayden was goading me. There's no doubt about that," said Gabriel. "But he was also making a point."

"He was telling us all that he could hurt me when and where he wanted," said Fate. "I'm a young Vampir, vulnerable. He could've snapped my neck and been out of here before you all arrived. But he didn't." She pressed her lips into a thin line.

"Exactly," Gabriel answered. He gave his head a sharp shake. "Much as I hate Drayden, I don't think he attacked you, Fate."

"How long until I'm strong, Gabriel? I'm sick of feeling like a sitting duck," said Fate on a sigh. She sat down on the edge of the bathtub and set her Glock down.

"Right now you're stronger than any of us when you dreamwalk, Fate, but on this side of reality, it will be a few years until you start to fully come into your Vampiric strengths."

She tipped her head back, closed her eyes and let a frustrated breath whistle past her lips. "I know."

Gabriel's strong hand braced her back. She opened her eyes. "Come, forget the mess in here," he said. "Forget what just happened. Let's warm your bathwater up."

"I'll leave you alone," said Adam. He turned and walked out of the room.

"Adam, thanks for being here," called Fate.

He stuck his head back in the room. "My pleasure, ma'am," he said with a cocky grin, and then shut the door.

Gabriel leaned across her and flipped the hot water on. Fate inhaled the scent of him. His cologne smelled great, but this was something different, *deeper*. It was his essential smell—pheromones, maybe. She didn't know. All she knew was that she was addicted.

Oh, man. She was addicted to him. Could she have gotten herself in any deeper?

He leaned toward her and kissed her. She sighed into his mouth and let him push her bathrobe off her shoulders. "Relax and get in," he said against her lips.

She slid to the side, lifted her feet onto the first step leading down into the depths of the large corner tub and descended into the water. "Ahhh," she sighed in contentment as the warm water enveloped her like an embrace. It felt perfect.

There was only one thing missing.

Fate watched Gabriel with sultry eyes. He sat on the side of the bathtub studying her with desire glimmering darkly in his gaze. She gave her best throaty *come-n-get-me voice* and moved languidly in the water. "Why don't you lose those clothes and come on in here? That would really relax me."

"Samantha and Niccolo will be here soon to share updates."

Fate moved to the side, reached out and grabbed his wrist. "Let them wait." She pulled and he came willingly. He slid right into the water, clothes and all.

He dunked his head under the water. When he came back up, he twined an arm around her waist and pressed her down against the steps beneath him. Skeins of his long black hair floated on the top of the water and his clothing pressed rough against her bare skin. "I can't resist you, Fate," he murmured.

"I thought maybe you'd shifted and your clothes were just an illusion," she said. "How did you get here so fast?"

"I was driving down the street toward the house when I felt the mental barrier breach."

She grabbed his lapels and wound her legs around his waist. "Well, right now, let's pretend they're an illusion and make them disappear." She pulled, causing the buttons of his shirt to pop off and the material to tear.

Laughing, he shrugged off the rest of his shirt. He leaned in toward her, rotating his hips so the rough material of his jeans rubbed just right against her clit and his chest brushed her bare breasts. "Impatient, aren't we?"

"For you? *Always.*" She tipped her head up and kissed him. "Make love to me, Gabriel." Her eyes widened. Had she just said...*make love*? That was a hell of a *faux pas*. Would he catch it? "I meant—"

He kissed her to stop her words. "I have every intention of *making love* to you, Fate. No request could sound sweeter to my ears than that one."

She opened her mouth to do some damage control, but someone knocked on the door. Fate groaned.

"Hey, Gabe," called Adam. "Samantha and Niccolo are downstairs."

"I'm coming," Gabriel called back. "Take a bath, *ma cheri*, and slip into bed. This will be *vite fait*, I promise. Quickly done. Especially if I know you're waiting for me." He pulled away and whipped his long wet hair back away from his face.

Fate just groaned again as she watched him leave her. He slid his wet shoes, socks and jeans off, toweled the excess water from his hair, and slipped his bathrobe on. Before he left, he leaned over the side of the bathtub and kissed her. "The thought of your hands running over your luscious body while you're washing will torment me when I'm downstairs."

She tried her best vixen smile. "Stay here and I'll let you watch, maybe even help."

"Believe me, I'll be back soon and when I do, I'll bring a surprise just for you."

She brightened. "A surprise?"

He laughed. "I think you'll like it."

After he left, she pulled his still floating shirt to her and hugged it. Even wet, her developing preternatural sense of smell picked up the scent of him still clinging to the material. She closed her eyes and inhaled.

No matter how much she tried not to be...she was head over heels in love with this man.

She was doomed.

* * * * *

Fate stood by the side of Gabriel's bed and watched him walk toward her. He'd been true to his word and hadn't taken long with Samantha and Niccolo. She'd taken her time in the bathroom and soon after she'd been finished, he'd come back up upstairs.

It had been long enough for her to do some thinking about her personal revelation, however. Fate didn't know when it had happened, but it had happened. And in the process, she'd left herself wide open for heartbreak and pain.

She just couldn't do it.

"Are you hungry?"

She nodded. The *sacyr* had retreated to a low, annoying hum within her. It was past time she should've fed.

"You cannot always take blood from me, you understand? We must vary in our feedings in order to satisfy the *sacyr*. Too much blood from one person can be dangerous."

"Well, I'll find a willing donor somewhere."

"No, don't bother. There is one arriving."

"Who?"

"You will see. Consider it room service."

"Uh—room service?" She looked away from him. "I actually don't think I should sleep in here anymore, Gabriel." She picked her pillow up from the bed and walked toward the door. "You've got lots of empty bedrooms. I'll just go find another."

His countenance darkened. He stalked to her, took the pillow from her, and threw it back onto his bed. It had all been done in vampire speed. Fate could only stand there and gasp in surprise. He cupped her cheek and stared down into her wide eyes. "Do you realize it's been close to four hundred years since I felt for a woman the way I feel about you, Fate?"

"I—uh."

"Do you know how many women I have been with during that time? I can't even begin to imagine the number. None of them, *not one*, has affected me the way you do."

He pushed her gently back against the wall, placing his palms flat on the wall on either side of her head, and covering her mouth with his. His tongue tasted so good against hers. So right. His knee parted her thighs and slid between to rub against her. Her eyes fluttered shut and, of their own volition, her hands came up to twine through the hair at his nape. She slanted her mouth to deepen the kiss.

She moaned as their kiss broke. "Don't—don't do this, Gabriel. You start touching me, kissing me, and I can't reason anymore," she murmured. "I can't think, or def—"

He replied by twining an arm around her waist and pressing his palm to the small of her back, so she arched toward him. He lowered his mouth and nibbled at her throat. "*Ma cheri*," he groaned. "I can't stop myself from touching you." He rubbed his thigh along her pussy, drawing a gasp from her. "I want to give you everything. I want you to have my all. Not just sex. But—*everything*. Do you understand?"

He pulled away from her throat and gazed at her. The look in his dark blue eyes was intense, consuming and full of deep emotion. She stood mesmerized by it. All she could do was part her lips and nod. It wasn't that she didn't understand. She just couldn't accept it.

That sinful gaze dropped to her mouth. He licked his lips. "Good, you comprehend what I'm saying. So now the only question is, do you *want* my all, Fate?"

Her eyes widened and she looked away. "I-I don't know what I want, Gabriel."

He cupped her chin gently and forced her gaze back to his. "I know you're afraid of this, of what we have between us. I know this has all gone very fast, and that you've been hurt before. I know *you*. Your fears, your desires, your fantasies. *Please*, my love, please know that as long as it's in my power, I will never hurt you or allow you to be hurt. Believe me. Trust me. Let me in."

Tears pricked her eyes and she blinked. They blurred her vision. She drew a shuddering breath. The sudden lump in her throat precluded her ability to reply.

"Don't answer me right now. Just-just let me take care of your needs tonight. Let me give you sustenance in all ways. Allow me to make another of your fantasies come true."

She looked at him. "What?"

He smiled mischievously. "I know them all. Remember?"

A choked laugh bubbled up from her constricted throat "How could I forget?"

He dropped a hand to her waist and the warmth of his skin bled through the sheer, silky material of her nightgown. It was another sexy one. He'd selected both the sexy ones from her apartment, and also the comfy, worn T-shirts and old boxers she liked to wear to bed. But Fate deliberately chose to wear the sexy ones, just to drive him crazy. She loved the fact he enjoyed her body in those revealing nighties.

He dropped his head and brushed his lips against her cheek and then went lower, to her throat. She felt the hard brush of his fangs against her soft skin and her heart rate sped up.

"Yes, Gabriel," she answered his nonverbal question. She closed her eyes, gripped his upper arms and tilted her head to the side to allow him better access.

Gabriel sighed into her throat and brushed his lips and teeth against her skin. At the same time, he worked his hand up under her thigh-length nightgown, gripped her panties and pulled. The fabric gave easily under his strength. He still wore his bathrobe, so she slid her hand between their bodies and undid the tie. She pushed the garment over his shoulders and off.

God, she was wet. Her pussy was creaming hard for him. Just the thought of him sliding into her put her on the edge of a climax.

He threw her panties to the side and slid his hands around to cup her buttocks, never moving his lips from her throat. "I need to taste you," he murmured raggedly against her skin. "I need to feel your hot, slick sex around my cock." He lifted her and she wrapped her legs around his waist.

The soft, vulnerable flesh of her core rubbed against the head of his shaft. He pressed her against the wall and slid it into her slowly, inch by delicious, mind-blowing inch.

She hit his shoulder with the flat of her hand. "Oh, dear God, *yes*," she moaned.

He seated himself within her to the base of his cock. As always, he stretched her to her limits with the length and breadth of him. Her fangs extended at the rush of sexual pleasure and the *sacyr* roared within her. She set her fangs to the smooth skin where his neck and shoulder met, ready to take as well as give.

"Do not bite me," Gabriel growled. "I know you're tempted, but you must have blood other than mine to satisfy the *sacyr*. We've already gone too long with you feeding from me with no variation. It isn't healthy for a new Vampir."

With a groan of frustration, she brushed her fangs against his shoulder, and then laid a kiss. "Bastard," she breathed.

She heard the smile in his answer. "By both birth and temperament, love." Cupping her buttocks in his hands, he started shafting her slowly up against the wall.

She closed her eyes. *Oh, dear, sweet...* "You're killing me, Gabriel."

"*Oui*, I plan on giving you more than just a *little death* this evening, Fate."

A shadow passed her closed eyelids and she opened them. Niccolo, dark, unconsciously seductive, and ever emotionally remote stood not far away. Besides his jeans, he was nude. No shirt and no shoes. But if this meant what Fate thought it might, he'd still get service. She was far too worked up not to allow Gabriel to bring to reality this the darkest of her fantasies, a *ménage a trios*.

She was sexually attracted to most of the Vampir that served Gabriel, though Niccolo was the most alluring to her in a base, purely physical way. Emotionally, though she was confused by her feelings, Gabriel was the only one she wanted. So, the thought of having the man she loved make love to her, and another man to whom she was highly attracted fuck her...

Well, now, could it get any better than that?

Niccolo stood silently nearby, watching them with a hooded, intense gaze—full of deep desire—as Gabriel drove into her over and over. Her gaze locked with Niccolo's and her climax teased her, flirted with her body.

Gabriel's fangs penetrated the skin of her throat and his glamour steamrolled over her, sucking her down into a hazy, lust-filled place of sexual satisfaction. As Gabriel began pulling on her blood, she came hard. The muscles of her vagina contracted and rippled around Gabriel's pistoning cock, and she keened out the pleasure that dominated her body.

Gabriel drew on her blood, extending her orgasm, and then finally raised his head. His gaze held Fate's as he asked, "What do you want, Niccolo?"

Fate looked at the other man across the room. Niccolo's pupils dilated, darkening his eyes to black. He held her gaze. "To taste her."

"As she will *need* to taste you," Gabriel answered. He lifted her away from the wall and bore her to the bed. The comforter was cool and soft beneath her body as he laid her down. His cock slipped free of her as he smoothed her nightgown up, over her head and off.

Gabriel shifted to her side and let his gaze rake her now nude body. Niccolo did the same at the end of the bed. She should've have felt exposed and vulnerable, but she trusted these two men. *Safe. Protected. Wanted. Aroused.* Those words better described how she felt as she looked from one man to the other, holding their gazes with her own.

"*Dio*, I want her," Niccolo said in a low, hoarse voice. He held her gaze as he reached down and undid his fly, slipped his jeans down and off. His long, thick cock stood up hard from a nest of hair as dark as what grew on his head. Uncircumcised like Gabriel, the skin of his cock was pulled back by his erection and Fate could see the strong veins snaking down the length, pumping blood to that beautiful organ.

Fate wanted to touch both their shafts. She yearned for both of them in her mouth. She suddenly realized she could indulge those desires. Nothing was stopping her. Gabriel had invited Niccolo here just to make that fantasy of hers come true. She smiled at them both, nearly purring out loud at the delicious revelation.

Before she could blink, Niccolo was there, straddling her body on the bed. His face came down toward hers. He brushed his mouth across hers once in a brief kiss. With a low growl, he descended stroking his sensual lips over her chin, her throat, and then her collarbone. Finally, he settled his mouth over her nipple, sucking and flicking at it with his tongue.

Gabriel's hand closed around her other breast and plumped it before he lowered his head and took her other nipple into his mouth. Fate's back arched as she threw her head back in pleasure, offering her breasts to the two men who now leaned over her.

Could there be anything better in the world than two gorgeous men sucking her nipples at the same time? At that moment, Fate doubted it.

Niccolo's broad hand planed her stomach and ran over her hip to her thigh. Exerting gentle pressure, he parted her legs and dipped in to stroke his fingers up her sex. Fate shuddered in ecstasy.

Niccolo broke away from her breast and trailed his tongue down her body. "A taste," he murmured as he lowered his mouth to feast on her sex.

At the same time, Gabriel moved up and kissed her deep and hard while he still played with her breasts, plumping them and teasing the sensitized nipples.

Niccolo parted her pussy lips with his thumbs and laved his tongue over her with several long, lazy swipes before settling down to suck her clit into his mouth.

Fate moaned long and low against Gabriel's mouth and groped between their bodies until her fingers wrapped around his cock. She stroked the length of him, found his foreskin at the base and used it to pump him. This time it was Gabriel who groaned raggedly.

Niccolo moved from her clit to suck her labia into his mouth. Using her own cream as lubrication, he drew a finger down to circle her nether hole. Fate jumped a little in surprise and both men soothed her back to relaxation.

"You will enjoy this, Fate," murmured Gabriel. "Don't shut yourself off to the experience. Open your mind to us."

Open her mind to them? Fate assumed they meant the telepathic pathways that worked when they desired them to. Tentatively, she opened her link to Gabriel. Pleasure trickled in. Pleasure at having her hand around his cock and his hand on her breast, to be sure, but also his deep satisfaction at allowing her to experience her deepest sexual fantasy and sharing her with a man he'd known for centuries. Gabriel trusted Niccolo with his own life, as well as her life, and he regarded him as a brother. The love and pride Gabriel felt coursed into her and warmed her. She closed her eyes and bathed herself in that light. Those feelings alone nearly brought her to orgasm.

Little by little, she opened the link fully. She left Niccolo's closed for now, happy enough to feel only what Gabriel felt.

Niccolo circled her anus again, awakening all the small nerves that surrounded it. Gently he pushed his finger in and thrust. At the same time, Gabriel sealed her mouth with his, consuming her gasp of pleasure. Niccolo slipped a second finger within her, widening her, stretching her muscles.

Gabriel reached down and stroked her clit. Pleasure suffused her and exploded outward. With a muffled cry, she came. Niccolo growled softly. He lowered his mouth to her and licked up the length of her sex, extending the tremors that radiated out from her core and lapping up the liquid of her climax. "You taste so sweet," he murmured against her swollen flesh.

After the climax had run its course, she pushed up. First, she turned to Gabriel and pressed the length of her body to his. Sliding her leg languorously between his, she kissed him deep and hard. She put every ounce of her feeling for him into her kiss and pressed her emotion through the mental link they shared. It brought tears to her eyes, this intense sentiment that welled up from the depths of her.

Perhaps she hadn't told him that she loved him, but she did. Gabriel could have no doubt about that now.

She'd just made sure he'd felt that stream of heavy and deep emotion radiating out from her.

He pulled away and stared at her, his eyes widening and his pupils dilating. His lips parted in shock. Then he wound a hand to the nape of her neck and pulled her to him for another lingering kiss. His palms rubbed her back as he kissed her, as though he just had to be touching as much of her as possible.

She finally pulled away from him, biting her lower lip and gazing at his cock, wanting to take it into her mouth. Raising her eyes to his, they connected. Silently she told him of her need to return the pleasure Niccolo had just given her.

There is no guilt in this, he answered. *I love you regardless of what happens here tonight. I invited this. I arranged it. And it arouses me to no end to see you so excited.*

Fate nodded and turned toward Niccolo. Lowering her eyes and giving him a sultry look, she crooked her finger at him. He crawled onto the bed toward her, his muscles rippling with every movement. His eyes were deep and dark, his expression intent.

On her.

She shivered at that look in his eyes. He had one goal here and she was it.

She put a hand to his hard chest and pushed him down to lie on his back. He went without complaint. Emulating what he'd done, she leaned over him and brushed her lips across his. His hand twined to the back her neck and he pressed her mouth to his. His hot tongue slipped into her mouth and he slanted his head to the side, deepening the kiss. Over and over he rubbed his tongue against hers. Her pussy tingled from the eroticism of the act.

When he let her free, she could barely breathe from the ferociousness of it. Such *need* had permeated that one simple, innocent act. On a psychic level, it opened up a pathway. She sensed him deeply now. It was as though he had a chasm within him. He needed someone to care for him, but day by day and little by little, the chasm was growing wider and deeper. Soon, no one would be able to bridge it.

She stared down at him in shock for a moment, suddenly understanding this man on a much deeper level, connecting with him in a far different way than she ever had before. This mutual understanding was something born purely from friendship and the simple act of caring for another living being.

She knew one thing—deep within, Niccolo hurt very much. It was real and raw and growing worse with every passing day.

Acknowledgement of her realization flickered through his eyes and then was replaced with dark lust. He pulled her down toward him again, angling his mouth for another kiss. She went without a whimper of protest.

Gabriel reached around her to cup her breast, rubbing the pad of his thumb over the nipple with agonizing slowness. It caused a new quickening between her thighs and broke the strange spell that coursed between herself and Niccolo.

Fate lowered her eyes and then her head. She flicked out her tongue and traced it over Niccolo's chest, licking up the salty tang of his skin and closing her eyes at the taste of him. Fate sensed and smelled the blood coursing through his veins. The *sacyr* within her raised its head and roared in response. She tamped it down with a supreme force of will. Other needs first, she told herself.

She found a flat nipple and laved over it like a cat. Niccolo's fingers twined through her hair and tightened as he groaned. She moved lower, kissing over his stomach and pelvis until she reached his cock.

Gabriel's hands found her hips and he positioned her rear toward him right before she engulfed the head of Niccolo's cock in her mouth.

Niccolo's hips bucked as she slid his length deep into her mouth to wet it. Fate wanted to purr at his response. It was heady to have two powerful Vampir so aroused for her. She slipped him out and ran her tongue just under the head of his shaft, licking and sucking at the sensitive place directly below it. He shuddered beneath her when she stopped teasing and slipped him back into the recess of her mouth.

Behind her, Gabriel urged her to part her legs. He slid his hand up her inner thigh to finger her labia and stroke over her clit. When she felt two of his fingers penetrate her pussy, she shifted and moaned around Niccolo's cock. She gasped when she felt Gabriel do the same thing at her anus. Slowly, Gabriel began to thrust in and out of both her pussy and anus in tandem.

She thought she'd lose her mind.

Fate parted her knees further and thrust her pelvis up, enjoying the slide of his thick digits in and out of her, possessing and pleasuring two powerfully sensitive erogenous zones at the same time. The feeling of being so filled—even if it was only by his fingers—was overwhelming and unbelievably erotic. The hot slickness between her thighs intensified as Gabriel kept up the torture.

Behind her, Gabriel growled, "Do you enjoy this?"

"Yes," she exclaimed breathily before she slid Niccolo's cock back into her mouth.

She sucked on Niccolo harder and faster until his big body tensed beneath her and he groaned, "*Dio. La vostra bocca è dolce.* Your mouth is heaven, so sweet." Relentlessly, she kept up the pace, adding a few exploratory touches to the mix.

Balancing on one elbow, she let a hand stray to caress his balls. Niccolo let out another groan when she fingered the sensitive place between his scrotum and anus.

Niccolo's body tensed and his hips bucked. She slid him far down her throat and that was enough to tip him over the edge. He let a low growl trickle between his lips as he climaxed. His hips thrust forward, and his fingers tightened in her hair. "Ah, Fate," he rasped. His hot essence shot down her throat.

Gabriel pulled her away from Niccolo with rough urgency, and positioned her in front of him on all fours. Gabriel parted her legs further and set the head of his cock to her anus. "Are you ready?"

Her fingers curled into the bedspread. She nodded vigorously. "Just fill me, Gabriel," she pleaded. "I need to be fucked." She was so turned on right now she was ready to explode.

Gabriel slid the head of his cock within her. She gasped at the exquisite mix of pleasure with the slightest bit of pain. She made a fist and punched the mattress. "Yes," she hissed, closing her eyes.

Inch-by-inch he fed her his glorious, thick cock until he was seated within her to the hilt. She never known it was possible to take a man so far into her this way, especially one as large at Gabriel.

Beside her, Niccolo's dark eyes filled with lust. His cock was already growing erect again. Niccolo shifted to lie beneath her. He cupped one breast in his large hand and palmed it, teasing the nipple. Then he licked over it and settled into sucking and drawing on it.

Fate hissed again, this time from the *sacyr* combined with the intense arousal battering her body. Niccolo's blood coursed thick, sweet and ancient just below her. That knowledge, along with the magic he wove over her breast was making her hunger near uncontrollable.

Gabriel chose that moment to begin to shaft her. Her fingers clutched the bedspread as she hung for dear life under Gabriel's thrusts. Any thought that went beyond his cock and its direct insertion into her body was eliminated.

Niccolo made a low noise in his throat. "Is he taking you the way you like, Fate?"

She nodded. A throaty, "Oh, yeah," was all the response she could manage. She could barely focus her gaze.

Niccolo rubbed his hands over her breasts and down her sides to her stomach. One hand stroked her sex, playing with her clit, petting and caressing.

Fate let loose a string of soft, unintelligible utterances.

Niccolo pressed a finger into her pussy, then another, all the while stroking steadily over her clit with his thumb. "Come for us," he drawled silkily as he began to thrust hard and fast. "Let go for us, Fate."

Gabriel's thick cock thrusting into her anus and Niccolo finger-fucking her pussy was more than she could take. Pleasure enveloped and exploded through her body, dominating her every muscle and her entire reality. She fought to stay upright and conscious as the deep, long waves pulsed over her.

Gabriel followed with an animalistic roar of completion. He thrust deep within and stayed that way. His cock jerked over and over as he released a stream come into her.

"Oh, God," was all she could manage. Her legs were shaky. Her whole *being* was shaky. She had a feeling she'd hurt in places she didn't even know existed tomorrow morning, but it would be worth it.

She lowered herself down onto Niccolo and wrapped herself around him. Fate nuzzled his throat and he tipped his head to the side as his arms came around her. "Feed," he murmured.

Her fangs lengthened at his command and the smell of the blood within his veins. She licked over his skin once, tasting salt and feeling the rasp of his five o'clock shadow on her tongue. Niccolo bent his head to her throat in the same moment, and she felt the brush of his fangs on her skin. He growled low and shifted a little to accommodate something Gabriel was doing. She felt Niccolo's cock rub against her — fully erect once again.

Gabriel's hands parted her legs. He licked her high on her inner thigh. The sensation of his fangs brushing her skin had her sighing in anticipation.

All at once, they bit, unfolding their glamour and coating each other within the heady, velvety folds. Sweet, beautiful, pleasurable pain momentarily flared at her throat and upper inner thigh. Niccolo's skin gave easily under her own bite and his blood coursed into her mouth, thick and hot and delicious. Just as she'd known it would be. It was a rich brew, made from an unknowable, uncountable number of feedings. It would not take much of it for her to gain what the *sacyr* required.

Niccolo rubbed against her and groaned deep his throat. The low sound vibrated through her, and his skin—hot velvet poured over steel—slicked over her breasts. Gabriel also moved. He ran his hand over her buttocks and rubbed her sex, stroking her clit.

Niccolo's fingers tangled in her long hair and brushed over her shoulders. She massaged the muscles of Niccolo's shoulders and back, occasionally dropping down to caress Gabriel's silky hair. The pleasure, as the two Vampir pulled on her blood, ebbed and flowed in tandem, almost as if they controlled it willfully and in cooperation.

And perhaps they did.

Her own skills at glamour were not so developed yet. She concentrated on keeping it steady for Niccolo, but that was all. As Fate began to think she'd had enough of Niccolo's blood, pleasure rippled through her, tingling at her nipples and vagina. It intensified and pulsed, almost causing her to lose hold of her own glamour and perhaps the hold she had on Niccolo's throat altogether. It was as if they both took her. Their hands, mouths, teeth and cocks worked phantom magic over her.

The glamour made it feel as though the experience was real. She felt Niccolo spread her thighs and slid his cock into her pussy. Gabriel took her from behind, using her own juices as lubrication. The dual penetration of their cocks overwhelmed her body and her mind. She felt the crush of their warm, muscular bodies sandwiching her.

Their cocks glided into her in a perfect rhythm, driving all thought from her mind. The musky scent of them filled her nostrils and the groaning, animalistic sounds of their pleasure filled her ears. She'd never felt so consumed in her life, had never felt so inundated by maleness.

The pleasure of the strong combined glamour flared hard and high. Fate lost her grip on Niccolo's throat, tipped her head back and keened out another climax. Both men held onto her as she came, feeding from her body as she convulsed in pleasure.

"Oh, God," she said again in wonder, once she'd come down a little bit from her physical high and both Niccolo and Gabriel had released their holds on her. Her vocabulary seemed limited this evening.

Niccolo chuckled.

"No, really. *Oh, God*," she said again in a satisfied, husky voice. "Have you guys done that often with women?"

Gabriel shifted and sat up. He pulled her toward him and lay back with her in his arms. Gently, he stroked her hair. "Not like this. Not as powerful as this, *ma cheri*. But, *oui*, over the years we have."

She yawned and nuzzled Gabriel's chest. "Do they ever have heart attacks?"

Niccolo sat up and then lay down near them on his back. "No, just orgasms," he said with a smile that didn't reach his eyes. "Lots of them."

She remembered then what she'd felt within him before she'd been caught up in the passion—the already deep and ever deepening sorrow within Niccolo. It was almost desperate, what she'd felt. Somehow, she'd unearthed the secrets he kept, had connected with a part of him he probably didn't want others to see.

Perhaps, in her refusal to open a mental link with him as she had with Gabriel, another type of psychic link had been forged? Likely, he would not be pleased that she knew what she did about him. He was on a precipice and needed a friend, needed help. But Niccolo wasn't the kind to ask for help, to burden anyone else with his "troubles" — at least that's how he'd think of it.

Fate sobered and snuggled against Gabriel, as though he could give her enough strength to broach the subject. "Niccolo, I—"

Niccolo turned and looked at her. Knowledge pulsed between them for a moment. No, he didn't want her to know. She snapped her mouth shut and bit her lower lip.

"Thank you for allowing me to share in your bond this evening. It was a true gift," Niccolo said. "There is strength between the both of you and much love. It strengthens me, in turn, to be a part of it if only for an evening, and if only on the very edge of it."

Fate smiled. "Believe me, the pleasure was all mine," she quipped, though her heart wasn't in it.

Gabriel let out a low snore. She and Niccolo smiled at each other, now in accord on many levels.

Eventually, her eyelids also became heavy and they slipped closed. Beside her, Niccolo also fell asleep.

Later, in the middle of the night, she awoke to a dark room. Niccolo was gone, but he'd covered her and Gabriel with a blanket before he'd left. She snuggled closer to Gabriel, grateful for his heat. In his sleep, Gabriel tightened his hold on her.

She drifted back to sleep and dreamwalked...

Chapter Nine

"I have a present for you." Gabriel pushed the box he'd tied with a red ribbon toward Fate. They sat together at the kitchen table drinking coffee, while in the living room various Vampir roamed. He and Fate caught their time alone when they could.

Her glossy mane of hair was mussed from sleep and tossed carelessly over a shoulder to trail down and cover one breast. She wore a short pink, silky bathrobe and small pink slippers. More than one of the guardian Vampir in the house had eyed her long, luscious bare legs as she'd come downstairs and headed into the kitchen. Niccolo was not one of them. It appeared he'd left the house early that morning.

Her large gray eyes widened as she spotted the box. "What this for?"

"Your safety. Open it."

She set her coffee cup down and picked the box up. With a flick of her wrist, she undid the ribbon and opened the top. "Ooooh, it's beautiful, Gabriel," she exclaimed as only a true gun lover could. Fate ran her fingers lovingly over the silver and black Beretta Bobcat that lay nestled in the sponge carton of the gun case.

She looked up at him. "But why? I already have a gun. Three, in fact."

"Yes, but none of those are small enough to fit into your purse, and—" he reached across the table for the box, picked up the gun and expelled the clip " — these are very special bullets, Fate. Niccolo got me in with someone who retrofits these for vampiric executioners." He handed her the clip.

She flipped it over in her hand, then pulled out a bullet and shrugged. "Well, the bullets look ordinary. What's so special about the gun?"

Gabriel shook his head. "The bullets might look ordinary, but they're not. There are small, very sharp bits of hawthorn branch in each."

She looked down at the bullet in surprise. "Oh."

"The casing is designed to splinter and break apart when it hits something, lodging the branch bit within flesh. Enough of those shot into an Embraced and they won't recover. I guess I don't need to tell you to be careful with them."

She inserted the bullet back into the clip and shook her head. "Nope."

"I wanted you to have something you could keep with you all the time. A weapon that'd be sure to kill any aggressor you may encounter while you're developing as Vampir."

"Thank you."

"I also wanted you to have this so that if anything ever happens to me, you'll be safe."

She looked up at him sharply. "Gabriel, you better never let anything happen to you, or I'll — " She snapped her mouth closed and looked chagrined. "You know what I mean."

He held her gaze for a long heartbeat, sending her intimate telepathic flashes of what they'd done the night before. She'd opened to him last night; let him feel everything she felt for him through that link they'd shared. Perhaps she'd never verbalized how she felt, but it'd been clearer than words last night.

And, good lord, she'd made him hot. Watching her work herself into such a sexual frenzy at having two men to pleasure her, two cocks at her beck and call. Watching her climax again and again, and then taking her blood and making her climax by his and Niccolo's glamour alone... He shuddered. It had been wonderful. His cock was even now growing hard as he remembered it all.

She caught his gaze. Her lips parted and her eyes widened as the images flooded her mind. Gabriel replayed just a snippet of the emotion she'd allowed him to feel. She looked down and away. "You know what I mean," she repeated meaningfully.

"I know what you mean, *ma cheri*. I wish you could say it." He reached into the pocket of his bathrobe and found another box, a smaller one, also tied with a red bow, and pushed it across the table toward her.

"Another one?" she asked in surprise.

"This one's pure pleasure."

She picked up the box, opened it and gasped. "It's lovely." Fate held up the delicate chain. A small white-gold raven charm sparkled in the morning light streaming through the bay window.

Gabriel stood and walked to her. He took the chain in one hand and moved her heavy hair out of the way with the other, and then draped the chain around her neck, securing it at her nape. "My transformational animal is the raven." He bent down and laid a kiss to her throat, drinking in the scent of her skin and her blood. "And you have transformed me for all time."

Fate stood and turned to him, winding her arms around his neck and compelling his head to dip so she could kiss him. "Thank you for the gun and the necklace, Gabriel. Thank you for protecting me. Thank you for making all my dreams and fantasies come true."

"The pleasure has been all mine, *ma cheri*."

She leaned back against the table and bit her lip. "Something troubles me deeply, Gabriel, about Niccolo. Last night, we connected for some reason. I didn't open any mental link to him. In fact, I kept it very tightly closed, but still—"

"Hmm. Perhaps it is your innate psychic ability shining through?"

"Maybe. All I know is that I felt Niccolo on a very deep level. For a moment, I knew his inner emotions, his deepest secrets. It was...not a nice experience." She glanced away and then back at him with concern etched clearly on her beautiful face. "Gabriel, Niccolo is in anguish."

Gabriel sighed. After a moment, he turned and walked to the bay window and looked out over his back yard. "Yes, I know that already. It's been a concern of mine for a very long time now, but I'm at a loss at how to help him. Niccolo is a hard man, one who does not admit vulnerabilities. I confess that it was my fear for Niccolo, as much as my trust in him that led me to invite him to our bed last night."

"What—what *exactly* is the trouble with him?"

"His soul is...fading. He has spent many years—centuries—stalking and killing, and it is starting to wear on him. It's beginning to *twist* him. He is starting to lose his capacity for—" He let out a sigh. "He's losing his humanity, so to speak. Though, being marked, he was never truly human."

"Why won't he stop being an executioner if it's affecting him so badly?"

Gabriel turned toward her. "You already know that Niccolo is very old, yes? Did you know he was once a gladiator?"

"Really? As in fighting for his life in a ring surrounded by people who paid money to see him die?"

Gabriel nodded. "He was a soldier serving under Emperor Nero, but something happened. We don't know what because he's never told any of us. It was something very bad, something he did. As punishment for his crime, they made him a slave. He was very strong, so it didn't take them long to figure out he'd do well in the ring as a gladiator. They were right, he was a star."

"But?"

"Niccolo was marked. One day his *mere de sang* found him and Embraced him and the day after, with his increased strength, Niccolo killed anyone who came within a foot of him and escaped the ring. That was in 62 A.D."

"Wow."

"His *mere de sang* showed him how to survive. They traveled together for centuries, until she was killed by a group of Vampir hunters. Niccolo hunted those men down one-by-one and finished them off. Then, heartbroken and lonely, he returned to Rome and stayed there. Eventually, he found others of his kind and they formed a community of Embraced. It wasn't long before an executioner was needed and Niccolo decided to render his services. The rest, well, the *rest* is history."

"I understand that Niccolo has been killing for a very, *very* long time, but you still haven't answered my question. You're the keeper, make him stop."

"I wish I could, but it's not so simple." He pushed a hand through his hair. "He tells me he doesn't know how to do anything else. Fate, you must understand that sometimes the realities we create for ourselves...they're unbreakable, unalterable. At this point, I'm afraid of what would happen if I somehow forced him to stop being an executioner."

"He left us last night."

"Yes, well, I'm sure he felt a bit of a third wheel, no?"

"Of course." She glanced away from him. "But we woke this morning to find he'd completely left the house." She shrugged. "Maybe my imagination is working overtime, but I'm afraid that seeing us, you and I, together, may have hurt him in some way. Maybe it reminded him of his own loneliness."

"I think you underestimate Niccolo's strength."

"I hope so." She turned and walked to the window. "I dreamwalked last night. I woke up in the early morning to find Niccolo gone and when I went back to sleep, I dreamwalked."

Gabriel took a step forward, his hand clenched involuntarily. He knew she could handle herself, knew that better than anyone, but that didn't stop him from worrying about her and feeling protective of her. He hated that she went up against the Dominion alone. "I'm sorry I wasn't there."

"It was fine." A smile flickered over her lips and she tipped her head to the side. "I fought the Dominion. Kicked some ass, too. My dreamwalking skills are enhancing with every trip I take to their realm as an Embraced."

He nodded. "Yes."

She licked her lips in an almost nervous gesture and glanced away. "I-I was transported somewhere strange, Gabriel."

He took another step forward. Why did she look so unsure of herself? "Where?" he forced himself to ask in a calm voice.

She held his gaze for a long heartbeat. "Dorian Cross's bedroom."

Gabriel lifted a brow. "Why do you think you ended up there?"

She shrugged. "I don't know, but the tones I told you about before? The tones were deafeningly strong there."

He ran his hand over his mouth and glanced away. "Interesting."

"Yes. I really don't want to suspect Dorian of anything, but—"

"But perhaps we should pay a little visit to Mr. Cross today?"

"Perhaps."

* * * * *

Fate watched Dorian's mansion come into view as their car crested the two-mile, poplar tree lined driveway leading to his front door. It was an elaborate white colonial affair that left the viewer in no doubt of Dorian's money, his place in the local community, or the world at large. After knowing how much money Gabriel had and how he never flaunted it, Dorian's house now gave her the impression of hopeless insecurity and perhaps overcompensation for small cock size, or something.

They parked the car and she, along with Gabriel, Charlie, and Niccolo walked up the front steps and rang the doorbell. When she'd called earlier, Dorian had been more than happy to schedule a time to fit her into his busy day.

Of course, she hadn't told him she'd be bringing her watchdogs, and she knew how much he loved the Embraced.

The maid, Betsy, opened the door and ushered them. Fate watched the middle-aged woman take in the three gorgeous men at her side. Charlie was dressed impeccably, as always, in an expensive dark suit. Understated silver cufflinks shone at his wrists. A hank of his glossy brown hair had fallen across his eye. With a twitch of his head, he flicked it to the side as he glanced around the marble and glass foyer. He probably felt right at home.

Beside her, Gabriel was dressed more casually in jeans, dark boots and a dark sweater. His long hair was clasped neatly at the nape of his neck.

Niccolo hadn't shaved this morning and had the beginning of a beard shadowing his strong jaw. It fit the feralness of his personality well. He, too, was dressed in a pair of jeans and a cable-knit sweater. They were an impressive pack of men, one sure to set any woman's pulse aflutter.

Fate hid a smile as Betsy glanced from one man to another, hardly knowing where to allow her gaze to linger. The housekeeper barely even took note of the woman standing in their midst. Fate was glad Adam hadn't come along; since Betsy's head probably would've exploded.

"This-this way, please," Betsy stammered. "Mr. Cross is expecting you."

She led them into a room filled with shelves of books, antique wooden furniture, and a huge oak desk. Dorian turned from the large window overlooking his property. "Fate," he started with a smile. His face fell as he took in her companions, his demeanor instantly turning icy. "You brought your new friends, I see."

"We won't allow her out of the house without an entourage these days," replied Gabriel tightly. "Nice to see you again, Dorian. This is Charlie and Niccolo."

"Hello, Gabriel," answered Dorian smoothly. "I believe I met your companions at a local gallery recently."

Gabriel inclined his head in response and smiled slightly.

Something moved in the corner. Fate glanced over to see Cynthia rise from her perch at a small corner desk and walk toward them. She was dressed in a burgundy business suit and high heels, and had twisted and secured her dark red hair at the top of her head with a long chopstick. "Hello, Fate," she greeted with a smile. Cynthia's gaze flicked to Gabriel and warmed. "Gabriel." Then she glanced at Niccolo and Charlie. "So nice to meet you."

"Hello, Cynthia," Gabriel answered smoothly. "Niccolo, Charlie, this is Cynthia, Dorian's right-hand woman."

"Would any of you like something to drink?" Dorian gave a nervous laugh. "Besides Cynthia or I, of course."

"He'd probably give us indigestion," murmured Charlie just loud enough for Fate to hear.

Fate stepped forward. "I'd love a whiskey on the rocks, Dorian."

"Excellent."

As Dorian prepared her drink, they seated themselves on the couch and chairs that rested on an expensive-looking navy and white area rug.

Dorian returned and pressed the whiskey glass into her hand, then turned and perched on a fragile-looking antique chair nearby. "So, Fate, what is it you needed to discuss with me?"

The thing was, she wasn't sure. She'd been transported to his bedroom last night when she'd been dreamwalking and the tones had been very strong there. It seemed to be some sort of a sign, but she couldn't be *sure* it was a sign. Things often happened in the world of dream that made no sense. Her being deposited in his bedroom last night could have been of those senseless things.

But her *gut* said otherwise.

And if she'd learned anything in her life, it was to go with her gut. So often that was where her psychic ability originated.

She took a long drink of her whiskey and caught Gabriel's eye.

Stalling, love? Gabriel asked telepathically.

Yep.

Don't know what to say or what you're even looking for?

Nope.

Maybe we should just make some meaningless small talk and leave. We haven't found any link to Dorian regarding your attack. He's just a rich man who hates the Embraced. Maybe your visit here last night simply occurred because of your association with him.

And the tones?

Gabriel paused. *I've never heard the tones. I don't know what they mean.*

They mean the Dominion is near.

She set her whiskey glass on the table in front of her and leaned forward. "So, Dorian. I'm told you're supporting legislation that might get me and my friends either hunted down and murdered in cold blood, or captured and dissected in a government lab somewhere."

Chapter Ten

Gabriel raised an eyebrow as he regarded Fate sitting there on the couch, a look of cool dislike momentarily passing over her beautiful features. Well, *that* had been subtle, he thought with a smile.

Looking uncomfortable, Dorian leaned back. "Fate, I—" A dark look passed over his face. Anger flared in his eyes. "I don't owe you any explanations," he snapped. "What political and social views I hold are no business of yours."

"They are when they endanger me and my family."

Dorian let out a laugh of derision. "Your *family*." He shook his head. "I knew from the moment I heard of your attack that you were lost to me forever."

"The Embraced and humans have been living together for eons," interrupted Niccolo in a low voice. "It is not impossible to believe we can interact positively."

Dorian stared at Niccolo and his gaze grew hard and cold. "Oh, yes, friendships and interactions between *predator* and *prey*. Wonderful." Dorian stood. "I think it's time for you all to leave."

Gabriel watched Fate rise and walk toward Dorian. A strange look had consumed her face. Her features were slack, her eyes lighted with some unfamiliar fire. Instead of walking, she almost seemed to float across the floor. If not for her eyes, he'd have said she was sleepwalking.

Fate approached Dorian with an intent look on her face. "You," she breathed.

Dorian stood and backed up into a statue that sat on a pedestal. He knocked it over and it crashed to the polished wood floor, but it didn't stop his horrified backward flight. "Wha-what's wrong with you, Fate? Your eyes are strange," he stammered.

"I can *see* you," she said. "You're in league with them."

A look of panic crossed his face briefly. He frowned. "With *who*?"

She cocked her head to the side. "The Dominion."

He glanced at Gabriel, then at Niccolo. The look on his face seemed...*guilty*.

Niccolo took a menacing step toward him, and then stopped in the middle of the room.

"N-no! You've gone insane, Fate. The attack, the Embrace, it's made you unstable," said Dorian.

She shook her head. "You are their human servant. They've promised you power and wealth if you help them gain control here. You've been helping to maneuver that bill through Congress on their behalf, according to *their* manipulations. They want the activities the Embraced curtailed. They—and you—want us extinguished from the face of the world, eventually. This is just the first step. They want to take over."

Dorian shook his head wildly. "You're raving, Fate!"

She backed him up against the wall, reached out and touched his cheek. "Poor Dorian. Don't you understand they're just using you? If you give them too much trouble, they'll suck you dry one night while you're sleeping...or worse. They'll manipulate you until you want to kill yourself, or someone else. They can do that, you know, and they will. They don't care about you."

Dorian closed his eyes for a moment, seeming to relax into her touch. Gabriel took a step toward them, but Niccolo put a hand to his chest to stop him.

"I loved you, Fate," Dorian whispered raggedly. "I never wanted you to be hurt. They told me to watch you, that you were special to them. They told me you could be an effective messenger for them, a liaison between this realm and theirs, and that I should keep you safe. I did what they requested, but at the same time, I gained a true affection for you. I-I wanted to help you with your art, grow close to you. I'd hoped that eventually you and I could..." He gave his head a shake. "But I never wanted you hurt."

Interesting. Dorian had cared for Fate. That had been why he'd championed her art so enthusiastically. Gabriel's thoughts churned. If Dorian was aiding the Dominion, Gabriel doubted he'd had anything to do with Fate's attack. The last thing the Dominion would want was for a powerful psychic dreamwalker like Fate to be Embraced and *grow* in her power.

No, this was an interesting and shocking revelation, but it had nothing to do with Fate's attack.

Gabriel ignored Niccolo's glance of warning and walked toward them. "Why did they want you to watch over Fate, Dorian?"

Dorian glanced at him, his eyes unfocussed. He blinked a couple times and seemed to register the question. "They wanted to seduce her over to their side. They said she had powerful abilities and that she could be of aid to them. But once she was Embraced, they…" He trailed off and looked back at Fate.

"I became too powerful and they wanted me dead," Fate said. "Didn't they, Dorian? That's why you were getting ready to arrange for a pack of hunters to come for me. You were going to send them on behalf of the Dominion, weren't you?"

It took a moment for Gabriel to register Fate's words. She must be picking up psychically on something in Dorian's mind. Rage started to simmer in the pit of his stomach.

Dorian squeezed his eyes shut and his face contorted in an expression of dread. "Yes," he whispered. "Yes…but I didn't want to do it, Fate. I didn't—I *don't* want you dead."

The rage simmering in Gabriel's stomach reached its boiling point. He moved across the floor with lightening speed and took Dorian by the throat. Gabriel's lip curled at the smell the fear rolling off the other man. "You're going to pay dearly for even thinking about it, Dorian, for anything to do with the mere *possibility* of Fate being harmed."

Dorian gurgled incoherently.

"We need him," said Charlie from across the room. "Gabriel, we need him alive."

"Leash your rage, Gabriel," said Niccolo sharply.

Out of the corner of Gabriel's eye, he saw Fate draw a sharp breath and take a step back, putting a hand to her head. Gabriel released Dorian and stepped toward her just as she fell backward. He caught her before she collapsed to the floor. Dorian chose that moment to dart to the side, headed straight for the door.

Niccolo moved with the speed only a very old Vampir could attain. He took him by the lapels of his expensive suit and slammed him up against the wall. "You're not going anywhere, Dorian," Niccolo spat. "You're in league with the very thing that could destroy your entire race. You're going to tell us everything we need to know. And you're going to do it *before* nightfall."

Gabriel was busy with Fate, but he heard Dorian's audible intake of breath as he realized why Niccolo demanded information *before nightfall*. *Ah, yes.* Likely the Dominion would not allow him to live now that he'd been discovered.

In his lap, Fate moaned and opened her eyes. "What happened?" she asked groggily.

He brushed his thumb across her forehead. "You went into some kind of a trance."

Fate's head whipped back and she screamed. Terror ripped through Gabriel at the sound of anguish that poured from her. Charlie came down on her other side. She quieted and breathed heavily in and out of her nose. Her eyes were wide.

"Fate?" Charlie asked. "Are you all right, Fate?"

Breathing just as heavy as she was, Gabriel laid his palms against her cheeks, as though he could stop whatever was happening to her. For her sake, he suppressed his rising panic. "What's wrong, Fate?"

"Intense shots of...of pain through my head." Her face contorted again. "Oh, God" She cradled her head in her hands. Gabriel held her against his chest as another episode passed. Finally, she lay still, but she breathed hard and shivered as though freezing.

She had two more attacks before she finally became calm and it looked like they had passed for good. Gabriel fisted his hands in her shirt. His knuckles were white. It was horrible to watch her go through each episode and feel helpless against whatever was causing them.

"The head pain might be an aftershock of your trance, Fate," said Gabriel. He tried hard to sound serene. "Are you all right now?"

Her face was pale and drawn. She nodded. "It was like a migraine, but ten times worse. I think they're over."

Gabriel pulled her up against him and scattered kisses over her face. "You scared me."

She kissed him back. "I'm okay. They're gone."

"You need to go back home and rest," said Gabriel.

She shook her head. "No. I'm f—"

"Fate," Gabriel said in a tone that brooked no argument. "You need to go home and rest."

Fate opened her mouth, and then bit her lip. "Fine."

"Good girl."

She reached out and grabbed Charlie's hand. "Will you take me back to the house? Gabriel needs to stay here with Niccolo and Dorian."

"Of course," Charlie answered.

"Are you sure, Fate?" asked Gabriel. "I can take you home myself." He tried not to let her hear the concern he felt. "I just want to make sure you're all right."

She glanced at him and nodded. "Take care of this business, Gabriel. I promise I'll be there when you get home."

Gabriel didn't want to argue. He just wanted Fate out of here. Somewhere safe. "Let me know if anything else happens to her, okay, Charlie?" said Gabriel.

Charlie gave a curt nod. "I'll take care of her." He helped her to her feet. "Come on."

Gabriel stood and watched Charlie gingerly lead Fate past Niccolo and Dorian who spoke in low, agitated tones by the wall. Fate looked so fragile right now. So vulnerable. So unlike Fate.

Gabriel shifted his gaze to study Dorian. The older man stood with wide eyes in front of a menacing-looking Niccolo. He looked like a cat trapped by a very large dog.

As Fate and Charlie left, Samantha and a SPAVA squad walked through the door. "What the hell is going on in here?" asked Samantha as she eyed Niccolo's undeniably antagonist posture toward Dorian.

Gabriel wondered for a moment who'd called in SPAVA, then remembered Cynthia. He glanced at her. She huddled in the corner, clutching her cell phone. He'd almost forgotten she was even in the room.

Samantha's gaze shifted from Niccolo to him. Her eyes narrowed. "Gabriel?"

"This is an internal matter, Samantha. It concerns the Embraced—" he flicked a meaningful glance at Dorian "—and the Dominion. SPAVA doesn't need to have anything to do with this."

Samantha took a step toward him, storms brewing fast and hard in her eyes. "Excuse me? Your *executioner* has *Dorian Cross*, one of the most powerful men in Newville, pinned to the wall of his own home. I think this is my jurisdiction!"

Gabriel pushed a hand through his hair and fought the rage rising within him. "*Dorian Cross* has admitted to aiding the Dominion," he bit off with barely controlled calm. "We have to undo the damage he has done. To do that, we must obtain more information."

Samantha turned toward Dorian. "Is that true? Did you admit to aiding the Dominion?"

Dorian nervously licked his lips, his gaze darting first to Gabriel, then Niccolo. "No. I don't know what he's talking about. They just barged in—" His sentence ended in a gasp as Niccolo threw him up against the wall.

SPAVA fanned out and closed around Niccolo. "Let him go," ordered Samantha.

"He's lying," growled Niccolo.

The SPAVA officers extended the hawthorn tips of their batons with an audible slide and click. Niccolo didn't move. He stared at Dorian, seemingly oblivious to the death that stood all around him.

"Stand down, Niccolo," said Gabriel.

"*No.* He's not getting away with this. I'll kill him before that happens."

Dorian didn't reply. He only stared wide-eyed. The scent of fear rolled off him in cloying waves.

"Don't make me order this, Niccolo," said Samantha in a husky voice. "Come on, we'll figure out what's going on together. Without violence."

Niccolo made no response. Several members of the squad raised their weapons. The tension that was already thick in the air grew heavier.

"Niccolo! Stand down!" commanded Gabriel. "He's not worth your life."

"Isn't he?" Niccolo hesitated for a long moment and then backed away. "No. You're right. He's not." Instantly, three SPAVA officers pushed him face-first against the wall. Niccolo could've thrown them all off with a flick of his wrist, but he didn't.

Dorian straightened his suit and scowled at Niccolo. Gabriel could hear the rapid beat of his heart all the way across the room. "That one, Niccolo, assaulted me. I want to press charges," declared Dorian.

"He barely touched you," said Gabriel. "If he'd wanted to hurt you would've done it."

Samantha shot him an icy look. "It's Mr. Cross' prerogative to press charges."

Niccolo turned toward Gabriel with a tired expression on his face. "Let them take me in."

Gabriel clenched his jaw as he watched the SPAVA officers cuff Niccolo's hands behind his back. With two officers on either side, they escorted him to the door. "I'll be in to post bail," Gabriel called after him.

"Take your time," said Niccolo.

Dorian went out after them, presumably to follow the squad car down to SPAVA headquarters and press charges.

Samantha turned to Gabriel before she left. For the first time in his experience of Samantha Ripley, her face was wiped clean of antagonism. She looked shaky, and even a little emotional. "I have to follow procedure, Gabriel, you know that. Doesn't matter what I might think personally of Niccolo or of Dorian Cross." She left, leaving Gabriel alone with Cynthia.

Gabriel turned and looked at her. He'd slept with her once about a year ago, though he remembered little of the encounter. "How much did you know about Dorian's involvement with the Dominion?" he asked her.

The scent of fear she gave off became stronger. Did he sound that menacing? Did she think he might hurt her? He forced a bland expression onto his face and relaxed the muscles of his body.

"Nothing. I knew nothing," she replied. "Swear to God. Dorian never showed any signs of being compelled by the Dominion."

Gabriel studied her. "But you spend every day with him. If anyone would be in league with Dorian, it would be you."

She closed her eyes briefly. "I swear, I knew nothing about it until today, Gabriel. I'm as surprised as you are."

"Can you tell me *anything*, Cynthia?"

She shook her head. "All I know is that Dorian started behaving strangely after Fate was attacked. He only started acting upset then." When she spoke the last sentence, her voice went almost imperceptibly lower and the metallic scent of fear flared to a hot smell of anger.

"How did he act differently after Fate's attack?"

"He was agitated, grieving, preoccupied...concerned." The scent of her anger turned to searing rage.

"Why would that make you angry?" he asked, making an effort to keep any sort of audible growl from his voice. There was something here, but what was it?

"Why do you think I'm angry, Gabriel?"

He tapped his nose and smiled. "One the tricks of the Embraced, Cynthia, love." He took a step toward her. "So, tell me."

She lifted her hands, palms out, in a gesture to ward him off. "No way, Gabriel." She shook her head. "That information is personal and my secret to keep."

What could be so sensitive that she didn't want to reveal? He took a step toward her and smiled. "Cynthia, you and I made love together once. Do you remember?"

She smiled back at him. "Made love? We fucked, Gabriel. You're so old-school sometimes, so silky and formal. Yes, we fucked. So what? It doesn't give you any special license to my personal life."

Ah, yes, there *was* something here, something totally unexpected. What was she holding back? He reached out and stroked his finger down her arm and made his voice like warm, seductive satin. At the same time, he unfurled his glamour over her, designing it to tempt her to open up, compelling and cajoling the truth out of her. "Fine, Cynthia. That's fine. You don't have to tell me. But if there's anything you ever want to talk about, you know I'll listen."

Her face contorted for a moment. "Wha—" she swallowed hard and sank down onto the couch. It was clear she was fighting the glamour, but she wouldn't win. He was far too strong.

Gabriel sat down beside her. "Are you angry with Fate for some reason?"

Cynthia's face contorted again and her mouth worked as she fought the spell of compulsion. "Dorian cares for her."

"Hmm...yes. Enough to send a pack of rabid Vampir hunters for her."

"I—didn't know about all that."

"You really didn't know about Dorian's involvement with the Dominion, did you?"

"No. If I had, I never would have—" She snapped her mouth shut and made a choking sound. Gabriel clapped her on the back. Choking on the truth, he'd make a guess.

Gabriel passed his hand over her face, intensifying the compulsion for her to speak her mind and feelings. "Don't fight the glamour, Cynthia," he murmured. "You'll hurt yourself. So, tell me. What wouldn't you have done?"

"That man who came to me, I never would've agreed to help him if I'd known I'd be thwarting all of Dorian's plans. I thought it was to my benefit, but even after Fate was turned—" she gave her head a hard shake "—Dorian still didn't want me."

Gabriel took her by the shoulders and turned her to face him. "What man? What are you talking about?"

"An Embraced. He came to me, said he knew that I was acquainted with you through your association with Dorian. He said he needed my help. Asked me to discover things about you and gave me lots of money to do it. I-I made myself *available* to you in order to get closer to you. But my plan backfired. We spent that night together, but you didn't reveal anything to me and you didn't want anything more from me afterward. So I was forced to follow you. That's how I found out about your interest in Fate."

Her face crumpled and she started sobbing. "I thought it was perfect. Xavier could Embrace Fate to get at you, and Fate would be out of the picture with Dorian."

Son of a bitch. He gave her a hard shake. "Xavier? Xavier *Alexander*?"

She let out a low sob and nodded.

He released her and stood.

"He came back to Newville yesterday morning expecting to find Fate a Demi," Cynthia wailed, hiccupping. "He's enraged that Fate made it through and ruined his plans. He's-he's planning on killing her. He's just waiting for a good time-time to spring."

"I'll deal with you later," he said in a chilly voice, and then went for the door.

As he went out the door, he trolled the mental links. *Charlie?*

No answer.

Fate?

Silence.

Xavier, you bastard, he broadcast at large.

Hello, Gabriel.

Gabriel stopped dead in his tracks. *Xavier?*

You were expecting someone else?

I thought you were dead.

Xavier laughed. *Those rumors have been greatly exaggerated.*

What have you done?

If you want to see your new love live to see another moonrise, you'll meet me at the empty warehouse on the corner of Grassley and Park.

You better not hurt her, you bastard. What did you do to Charlie?

I'd come now, if I were you, Gabriel.

The mental link slammed shut.

Gabriel began to run.

Chapter Eleven

Fate's eyes flickered open and she moaned at the pain in her head. Her head had pounded and ached *before* she'd been knocked unconsciousness, goddamn it.

That Vampir had come out of nowhere. One moment Charlie had been helping her out of the car in front of Gabriel's house, the next moment Charlie had just been...*gone*. In the space of a heartbeat, she'd felt something massive hit her head and that'd been it.

She blinked and squinted, taking in her situation. Her wrists and ankles were tied and she was lying on her side...on something hard and pokey. Her eyes widened. On her *gun*. The one with the hawthorn bullets. She'd slipped into her coat pocket before they left the house that morning. Too bad there was no way in hell she could reach it.

She blinked again and examined her surroundings. A huge storage room met her gaze. Crates and metal equipment stood scattered around on the concrete floor. Several large metal walkways crisscrossed far above her head. Was it a factory? A warehouse, maybe?

She moved her head and winced. Charlie lay nearby, still out cold by the looks of it. He was also bound at the ankles and wrists. Blood crusted his hair and the right side of his head.

Silent and swift, a shadow passed over her. Then a man—the Vampir—was suddenly kneeling beside her. He reached out and lovingly brushed a stray hank of hair away from her face. "Remember me, Fate? Maybe not, hmmm?"

"You-you're the one," she sputtered. She could feel intuitively that this was the Vampir that had attacked her.

"Yes, I'm the one." He had the barest trace of a French accent.

"Don't hurt Charlie."

He laughed. "How noble of you. I'd be more worried for your own skin." He produced a long, thin black stick and waved it at her. Fate sucked in a breath, recognizing the instrument instantly as a hawthorn baton, like the ones SPAVA carried. "Do you know who I am, Fate?" he asked.

She shook her head.

"My name is Xavier Alexander and I'm a very old friend of Gabriel's. Did he tell you about me?"

"Yes." He pronounced his name *Egs-ah-vi-yay*, the same way Gabriel did.

"Good. Then I don't have to recap."

He pressed a button on the end of the baton and the hawthorn tip extended. He stroked it down her cheek, and Fate closed her eyes and shuddered. "Tch, tch. You weren't supposed to make it the whole waaaay," he singsonged. "I never would've guessed you'd make it through the Demi."

She opened her eyes to slits and swallowed hard. "I'm full of surprises," she rasped. At the same time she said the words, she brought her knees forward and pushed him off balance. She jerked her head back to prevent the baton tip from scraping her shoulder as Xavier toppled to the side.

He sat up from his sprawl and stared her down. "Bitch," he murmured. "Don't play games with me. I'm not planning to kill you until Gabriel gets here, but I might change those plans if pushed."

The metal door of the warehouse slammed open. "Well, we wouldn't want that, would we?"

Xavier stood and turned slowly. "Gabriel."

Gabriel strolled toward them slowly, glancing at Charlie and Fate. *Are you all right?* he asked Fate mentally.

So far, she replied.

And Charlie?

I don't know.

Gabriel smiled tightly at Xavier. "Long time, no see. I thought you were dead, Xavier. Too bad I was wrong."

"I arranged all that. I wanted you and Laila to think I was dead so that I could disappear with no questions."

"Then why the *hell* are you back?"

"Tch, tch. No, no, Gabriel. You misunderstand me. I never really left. I've been waiting and watching all this time. Waiting for you to care about someone more than you care about yourself. I wanted to pay you back for Laila. I wanted you to have to watch her—" he nudged Fate with his foot "—be Demi."

Fate laughed. "That didn't exactly work out for you, did it?"

"Why are you blaming me for Laila, Xavier? You know as well as I do that there was no way I could ensure she'd become fully Embraced."

He turned his head and spat. "You slept with her, Gabriel. I know you did."

Gabriel narrowed his eyes. "Lots of men have slept with Laila, Xavier. It's how she *survives*. And we thought you were dead, remember?"

"*I know that's how she survives*," he roared. "Goddamn it, I watched her, the woman I loved, flit from bed to bed until I couldn't watch anymore." He knelt, pulled Fate's coat open, and ripped the seam of her shirt, opening up the side and exposing her skin. She closed her eyes and gasped.

Gabriel took several panicked steps forward.

Xavier placed the baton tip to her side and caressed her skin with it — back and forth, back and forth. Gabriel took another few steps. Xavier held up a hand, palm out. "Not another inch closer, lover boy."

"Xavier," Gabriel growled in warning.

"You were supposed to watch Fate do the same thing Laila did. Fate was supposed to fuck other men to survive, all the while making you crazy with jealousy and eventually contempt and hatred."

"Why, Xavier? *Why* is your rage and need for vengeance fixated on me? You begged me to Embrace Laila and I did. It's as simple as that. You both knew the risks. You knew the cost if she didn't make it the whole way. You can't hold me accountable for what happened."

"But you slept with her, over and over, night after night."

"You were gone, Xavier. Long gone. She came to me. She asked me to share her bed. Laila was alone without you." Gabriel shrugged. "I'm truly sorry, Xavier. I never would have slept with her if I'd known you were still alive."

Xavier's voice shook with emotion when he spoke next. "She fell in love with you."

Ah, thought Fate. So was that the reason for all this. Heartbreak, surely, the kind that lasts a lifetime, but perhaps *jealousy* even more so. Cold, hard, unquenchable jealousy.

"I have no control over Laila's feelings, Xavier, but I do not return them. I never have."

The door at the far end of the warehouse opened. Gabriel turned to watch Laila walk through it. Above her, Fate heard Xavier's breath hiss out of him. The baton scraped her waist in his inattention and she cringed and squeezed her eyes shut.

"*You* left *me*, Xavier," Laila called from the door. "Remember? You wanted me to spend all eternity with you, then you left me when I did what I had to do to survive." She gave a bitter laugh. "Now I find out you faked your death just to get away from me." She'd heard the whole thing with her preternatural hearing, probably.

"To get away from having to watch you fuck every man and woman who came along," Xavier answered.

"The others meant nothing, Xavier. They were just sustenance. They were only food. I *loved* you."

Above Fate, Xavier hissed in response. The hawthorn tip of the baton brushed dangerously hard against her, almost scratching her skin. She cringed again and shared a glance with Gabriel. His Adam's apple worked as he swallowed hard. He was every bit as frightened as she was.

"Did you bring Laila here?" Xavier demanded of Gabriel.

Gabriel spread his hands and shrugged. "I thought your issues might have more to do with her than with me. I thought maybe you two had things to talk about."

"Bastard."

"I was a friend once."

Xavier snorted. "Once. A very long time ago."

"Please stop this insanity, Xavier," said Laila. She glanced at Fate. "Let her go."

"You should want me to kill her, Laila," Xavier said. "Your way with Gabriel would be clearer then."

Laila shook her head. "I couldn't make Gabriel love me, no matter how hard I tried." She looked up at him with eyes wet with unshed tears. "I couldn't make you love me either."

"I never stopped loving you," Xavier answered.

By this time, it seemed Xavier had almost completely forgotten about Fate and the weapon he had pointed at her. The baton he held wavered, but this time away from her. It lifted an inch, and then another. Fate breathed a little easier. Possibilities for escape ruffled through her mind.

Fate shared another glance with Gabriel. *Be ready*, she said to him in her mind.

Fate, no!

She took advantage of Xavier's distraction by lifting her bound legs and torso from the floor and pivoting hard and fast on gun in the pocket of her coat. The metal bit painfully into her hip. Her legs swung just enough to knock Xavier off balance.

He went down hard.

All hell broke loose.

With a snarl, Gabriel leapt on Xavier. They rolled, punching and fighting. Xavier tried to stab Gabriel with the baton, making Fate's breath hitch in her throat with fear, but Gabriel grabbed Xavier's wrist and forced him to drop the deadly weapon.

When they rolled away from the baton, Fate started to inch over with the intention of kicking it under a huge piece of machinery that stood nearby.

Laila just stood there and screamed.

When she reached it, Fate maneuvered her heels over the baton and tried to push and scrape it over the concrete floor, but with bound ankles, it was slow going.

Suddenly, Xavier was on her. He grabbed the baton and raised it over his head, ready to plunge it straight down into her stomach. Her gaze focused on the tip, and her mind stuttered numbly over the fact that she was about to meet her death.

Then Xavier was just…*gone*.

Fate watched Xavier fly through the air like a lawn dart. He slammed violently to the floor not far from Laila. The impact made him slide along the floor on his back for a distance. Finally, he came to stop, still clutching the baton.

Fate glanced up to see Gabriel standing over her with his hand raised toward Xavier. His lip was bloodied and gashes marred his face.

She looked back at Xavier. A look of rage and hatred had contorted his face into a hideous mask. He stood and raised his hand, palm out, toward Gabriel. Gabriel rose above the floor a few feet, but didn't move any further. Xavier screamed something in French. His face reddened and the veins in his neck stood out prominently as he exerted himself.

Gabriel looked nonplussed. He did a graceful back flip in the air and descended to the floor. He shrugged. "I was always better at that than you."

"Bastard," Xavier raged.

"I think we've established that," Gabriel replied calmly. He knelt and undid the bonds around Fate's wrists.

Xavier took a step forward. "Get away from her, Gabriel. She's mine now."

Gabriel paused and looked up at Xavier with a cold expression on his face. It made even Fate want to scramble away from him. Here was the strong, ruthless Vampir who'd both gained a territory and kept it. "You're no match for me, Xavier. This mission was a suicidal one. You know it, and so do I."

Xavier turned and stared at Laila. She gasped, and then turned to run. Xavier stalked toward her, baton in hand.

"No," Fate screamed. She fumbled, trying desperately to draw the gun from her pocket.

Gabriel raised his hand to lift and toss Xavier once more, but he wasn't fast enough. Xavier slashed his arm down, slicing Laila's back open with the baton. Her clothing tore under the sharp tip. Her skin ripped. She screamed and went down as her blood began to run hot and heavy. The smell of it filled the room. It attacked Fate's nostrils with its cloying scent and made bile rise up in her throat.

Fate drew a sharp breath and squeezed her eyes shut. Poor Laila. She'd had such a hard life. She'd deserved happiness and caring from someone, not to meet a violent end at the hand of a man who'd professed to love her.

Gabriel growled low in his throat and then emitted a bone-chilling snarl. He raised his hand. At the same time, Xavier lifted from the floor and flew across the room to slam brutally into the far wall. He slid down, moaning, and Fate saw his body had impacted the wall itself. The concrete crumbled where Xavier had made contact.

Xavier stayed down, looking like a bit of crumpled paper thrown on the floor. Fate shuddered in relief.

Gabriel helped her into a sitting position and undid the bonds around her ankles, and then kissed her long and tenderly. "I've never been so afraid, Fate. Never," he murmured.

"I love you, Gabriel," she whispered hoarsely. She set her forehead to his. "I love you. I love you," she said over and over.

He kissed her again. "I know. I'm glad you said it."

Gabriel moved to untie Charlie, and Fate worked the blood back into her feet and stood. She spotted Laila lying on the floor. The Demi woman was now silent and still. Fate choked back a sob and started across the room toward her. From the corner of her eye, she saw movement and stopped in her tracks.

Xavier stood slowly, a look of resignation on his face.

"Fate, get back," called Gabriel.

She pulled her gun from her pocket, raised it, and trained it on Xavier's chest. "I'm okay, Gabriel," she said evenly.

Xavier stared at Laila for only a heartbeat or two, before he turned and fixed his killing gaze on Fate. He raised the baton and stalked toward her.

"Monster," Fate breathed. "I'm not going to miss this time." She shot. The bullet took Xavier in the shoulder. He paused, but kept coming. Fate shot again and hit him high in the chest. Still he came toward her like a deranged locomotive. Fate opened up, pounding round after round into him.

Finally, Xavier stumbled and gasped, his eyes opening wide. A look of shock overcame his face as the hawthorn began to do its thing within his body. He tripped, and then fell forward. He slid across the floor on his chest toward Fate and came to a stop with the crown of his head touching the toe of her shoe. The hawthorn baton went limp in his hand, just brushing the hem of Fate's coat.

Everything went silent.

Fate let her gun clatter to the floor. Her heart thumped so hard in her chest, she thought maybe it would break through her rib cage. She dropped her head back and raggedly let out the breath she'd been holding. A warm hand closed around her wrist, startling her. She opened her eyes, saw Gabriel, and registered the fact that his face was a mass of blood and bruises. One of his eyes was swollen shut.

She allowed him to pull her into his arms. "Are you all right?" she murmured into his chest. His blood soaked hot through her clothing and branded her skin.

"I'm fine, *ma cheri*. Just fine now," he rasped. "Already beginning to heal with you safe in my arms."

Shuffling noise drew Fate's attention. Charlie had recovered consciousness and had spotted Laila. "*No*," he said hoarsely as he struggled to stand.

"Are you all right?" Gabriel asked Charlie.

Charlie didn't answer. It didn't appear he heard or saw either of them. One person alone claimed all his attention. He staggered across the room and knelt beside Laila.

A lump formed in Fate's throat as she watched him take Laila into his arms and rock her back and forth. It was perfectly clear from the tenderness with which he held Laila and the look on his face that Charlie had cared very deeply for the woman.

"Charlie—" Gabriel started gently.

"Leave," Charlie snapped. "Take Fate and get out of here. Leave me alone." Cold, barely leashed fury laced his tone. It startled Fate, made her jump in Gabriel's arms. Charlie sounded like he'd kill them both and not think twice.

Gabriel stood looking at Charlie as if suddenly comprehending what she had just realized. "I'm—" he started.

"Leave," Charlie roared. The whole building vibrated under the force of emotion emanating from him.

Fate touched Gabriel's arm. Together they walked out of the warehouse and into the cool evening.

Chapter Twelve

Gabriel stared at Samantha and the three SPAVA officers that flanked her, as they stood in his entryway. "You know that isn't true," he said.

Samantha narrowed her green eyes at Gabriel, and Gabriel stared right back. Finally, she looked away. "I don't know what's true. I know what I want to believe, and I know where the evidence points." She looked back at him. "And I gotta follow the evidence. That's my job, remember?"

After the event at the warehouse, he and Fate had gone straight in to bail Niccolo out of jail. They'd been coated in blood, and had been bruised and battered, but Gabriel had wanted his friend free so badly that he hadn't wanted to stop and take time to clean up. Instead, Fate had received her first lesson in glamour, and had cast an illusion that made them appear blood and injury-free.

After they'd told Niccolo about what had happened, Gabriel and Fate had gone home to clean up and have a nice long night's rest, the first totally peaceful one since Fate's attack. Niccolo had gone home to his apartment, they'd assumed.

This morning they'd awoken to the morning paper trumpeting the premature death of Dorian Cross and his assistant, Cynthia Hamilton. Both had been found slain in Dorian's bedroom.

"Niccolo had a motive," Samantha said. "The whole SPAVA squad saw him threatening Dorian Cross yesterday afternoon, Gabriel. That is an undeniable fact. There were no fingerprints to be found and the strength that was used to murder them—" she shook head and shivered "—it was preternatural, Gabriel. It was Vampiric."

He pushed a frustrated hand through his hair. "It was the Dominion, Samantha, *the Dominion*. They knew that Dorian's usefulness had come to an end and they killed him. Cynthia was there and in the way, so they took her too."

"So, I'm supposed to believe a group of incorporeal entities, the bogeymen of dreamland, murdered the most powerful man of Newville and his assistant, and did it all to make it look like Niccolo did it?"

Gabriel clenched his jaw and felt a muscle twitch. "I don't know about that last part. That could be coincidence. But, more or less, yes."

She rolled her eyes. "I have no time for fairy tales, Gabriel."

"That's good, since this isn't one. The sooner everyone begins to believe the Vampir are telling the truth about the Dominion, the better."

"Niccolo has done a whole lot of killing in his life, hasn't he? Isn't it possible the line has blurred a little for him? Maybe he can't tell the innocent from the guilty anymore? Maybe somehow he thought Dorian and Cynthia were guilty? Maybe he thought he was just doing his job?"

"They *were* guilty, Samantha. Dorian was aiding the Dominion and Cynthia helped to organize the attack on Fate. Even so, Niccolo didn't do this."

"Where is he?"

He spread his hands. "I don't know."

She stared at him. "If you did know, would you tell me?"

"No."

She blinked. "I hope I don't find out you're harboring a fugitive, Gabriel."

He smiled sweetly. "I hope you don't find Niccolo, Samantha."

Something dark flickered through her eyes. "Life in prison is a very long time for an Embraced."

"Especially an innocent one."

They stood for a long heartbeat, holding gazes. Samantha jerked away first and turned. "C'mon, we're wasting our time here," she said to her men.

Gabriel leaned against the doorjamb and watched them walk down the porch stairs to their cars. As their vehicle pulled away from the curb, Gabriel looked up at the blue, cloudless morning sky.

And he'd thought they'd wake up trouble-free today. How naïve of him.

Another car pulled up to the curb, and Gabriel lowered his gaze to watch Adam get out of his silver SUV and bound up the walkway toward him. "He's gone, Gabe. G.O.N.E. in all caps, *gone*. When SPAVA searched Niccolo's apartment this morning, it probably didn't look like he picked up and left, since all his clothes and stuff are still there. But the few things I know mean something to him? I checked for those and they're *gone*, man. Kara is gone, too."

"I can't feel him anywhere close, Adam. And he won't respond when I troll for him mentally." Gabriel sighed, partly in relief, partly sorrow. "Yes, he's gone."

"I know that Niccolo was having some problems, but he didn't kill Dorian and Cynthia," Adam said. "That's just not him." He sounded like he was trying to convince himself.

"I *know* he didn't do it, Adam. He probably heard about the killings on the news this morning, figured everything pointed straight at him and fled."

Adam ran a hand over his stubbled chin. "Makes him look damn guilty."

"It's good he ran. They'd convict him, Adam. SPAVA knows he had a motive, and I highly doubt Niccolo's got an alibi. SPAVA heard him threaten Dorian yesterday with their own goddamn ears. Anyway, they're always dying to send up an Embraced." Gabriel shook his head. "Niccolo wouldn't stand a chance."

Gabriel and Adam turned at the sound of footsteps on the stairs. Fate descended, wearing a short white bathrobe. The bruises on her face, where Xavier had struck her, were already beginning to fade. A good night's sleep had taken care of them. As an older Vamp, his had healed hours after they'd been inflicted.

She sat down on the third step from the bottom. "He said to tell you he'll be okay and he'll see you soon. He took Kara and went back to Italy."

Gabriel frowned. "Did he contact you?"

She nodded. "He didn't mean to, it just happened. I think it's a combination of my developing psychic ability and the fact we connected so well —" she glanced at Adam "—uh, that night. He said to tell you he didn't do it."

"There was never any doubt," said Gabriel.

"Damn. First Charlie, now Niccolo," muttered Adam.

Gabriel looked at him sharply. "What do you mean? Where's Charlie?"

"Charlie took off this morning, too. He took Laila's death really hard," answered Adam.

"Where did he go?" asked Fate.

Adam shrugged. "He wouldn't say. He just said he needed to get away for a while, then lit out."

"Nice for him to let me know," Gabriel ground out.

"Let him have his time away, Gabriel," said Fate gently. "He was in love with that woman, Laila. Think how you'd feel if I'd been the one to take that hawthorn tip last night."

"Please don't say that, Fate," he answered.

She gave a slight smile. "See?"

"Point taken."

"He said he'd be back soon, Gabe," finished Adam. He touched his forehead the way he did from time to time, as though he wore a Stetson. "Well, I just stopped by to see how you were. I've got work to do, so—"

"Thanks, Adam," said Gabriel.

"For what?"

"For all you did for Fate and I through this whole thing. You've been great. I was a fool to ever consider demoting you."

Fate stood, walked to Adam, and gave him a hug. "Yes, thank you so much, Adam."

Adam grinned and winked at her. "Well, I kinda like you both." He gave Gabriel a gentle punch to the upper arm. "Anyway, you have to say that, seein' as how you don't have anybody left around here to fill my boots if I were demoted. Take the day off, Gabe. You have the house to yourselves for once. You can get up to five different kinds of mischief and there's nobody here to walk in on you." With another wink, he strolled out the door, whistling.

Gabriel closed the door and Fate fell against his side. "Laila, Charlie, and Niccolo, all in twenty-four hours," she said softly. "I feel like I've lost family. I'm even grieving Laila and she hated my guts."

He nuzzled the top of her head, breathing in her scent. "Niccolo and Charlie will be coming back. They'll be fine."

"I hope so." She sucked in a breath. "And Dorian and Cynthia," she moaned.

"Uh, Fate? Dorian and Cynthia both betrayed you. Cynthia helped Xavier target you, and Dorian was planning to set a pack of Vampir hunters on you. Are you actually grieving them?"

She raised her head and shrugged. "I haven't decided yet. I think everything is just starting to register. Lots of things happened very quickly yesterday."

"I know." He pulled her close and kissed her. "I was afraid I'd lose you."

She laughed. "I was pretty afraid you were going to lose me, too."

"I never, ever want that to happen, Fate."

She sobered and rubbed her lips against his. In a husky, seductive voice, she said, "And *I* never want to lose *you*."

He slid his hand between them and undid the thin silk belt of her bathrobe, reached in and caressed her waist.

* * * * *

Fate closed her eyes and enjoyed the feel of Gabriel's hand on her skin. It felt so much better than the tip of a hawthorn baton. God, she was glad to be alive today. Although the sheer joy of her survival was tempered by the sorrow she felt.

For Laila. For Charlie. For Niccolo.

Gabriel reached up and cupped her breast. Maybe for a while she could drown herself in the fire that was Gabriel. He seemed to be offering respite from her swirling, confusing thoughts and emotions. And she'd take it. She'd take anything Gabriel wanted to give her. He'd protected her, and then risked his life for her. Those were two things Christopher never would've done.

Yes, she loved Gabriel very much. She loved him far more than she feared being hurt or rejected.

Far more than anything at all.

He drew her against him and stroked her back, her hair, her derrière and her breasts. Fate leaned into him, enjoying the sensation of his hands on her body. She rubbed her palms up his arms and over his shoulders, kneading and caressing his muscles.

When she tipped her face toward him, he kissed her long and deep. He rubbed the nape of her neck with strong fingers, and brushed his lips back and forth across hers, igniting a little fire between her thighs.

"Lay down, love," he purred in her ear.

"We're in the entryway, Gabriel," she murmured. "Maybe we should move this upstairs."

He gave a low, trickling growl. "I'd take you in the middle of Times Square at noon on a Wednesday at this point." He thrust his hips against her so she could feel the proof of his arousal. He pushed her off balance and eased her down to the floor.

Gabriel knelt beside her and parted her bathrobe. He looked down at her with a heated gaze. It traveled from her face, down her body to the patch of brown curls covering her pussy. His hands soon followed. He traced his fingertips from her throat, down her breasts to her calves and back up again. He did it reverently, with a gaze filled with love.

Fate sighed happily, enjoying every moment of it.

"Part your legs and bring your knees to your chest, so I can see—" he gave her wicked grin "—*everything*."

She stretched her knees back and up as he'd requested, feeling wanton as hell and loving every second of it. He ran his fingers over her folds and slipped a finger within her. With the index finger of his other hand, he massaged her clit in a circular motion. She tipped her head back on a moan.

He inserted a second finger to join the first and kept stroking her clit. She dropped her head back to the rug covering the wooden floor, arching her back and stabbing her tight nipples into the air. She could feel how wet she was becoming. All she wanted was for him to slide inside her.

A warm tongue replaced his finger on her clit, but he still thrust his fingers in and out of her. Gabriel groaned and it reverberated through her whole body. He spoke so his lips brushed her clit. "You taste good, Fate." He laved her clit with the flat of his tongue.

"You're killing me, Gabriel," she breathed.

The tease didn't answer her. He removed his fingers from her pussy and swept his tongue over her, drawing her labia into his warm mouth and sucking on them. His tongue played with the entrance of her vagina, then thrust within it.

She let out a strangled cry and her body tensed. The pleasure was building, cresting toward climax. Gabriel stopped right before she reached it and she tipped her head up, looking down her body at him accusingly. "You better be bringing that cock over here right now, Gabriel Letourneau," she snapped.

He grinned at her. "Patience, love." He undid the belt to his own bathrobe and let it fall to the floor. Fate drank in her fill of his luscious, naked body. He stood looking down at her and stroking his cock with one hand. The sight made her catch her breath in anticipation.

He knelt and placed his shaft to her passage. The smooth, rounded plum-shaped head pushed at her, taunting her. He slid it up her pussy until it brushed against her clit. She whimpered. "No more teasing, Gabriel. Come inside me."

He moved his shaft against her, but did not slip inside. "Not yet. I want you crying, begging for me to take you. It's torture for me, too. I want to slide inside you and thrust until you come all over me."

"Oh," she moaned. "I want that too. Let's do that instead of teasing."

He chuckled. "Tell me again you love me."

Her head snapped up. "What? Are you bribing me with the promise of an orgasm again?"

He nodded. "Yep."

"You're evil. *Evil!*"

"So you've told me." He helped her to sit up and turn over on her stomach. "Raise that pretty ass into the air, love," he whispered into her ear.

She pushed her hips up, feeling exposed and *very* turned on. He stroked over her sex until she purred, then plunged two fingers into her pussy from behind, driving her hard and deep over and over. She gasped and then moaned. Her fingers dug into the carpet as a long, hard climax flirted with her body.

Gabriel stopped.

She let out a whimper of frustration, made a fist and punched the carpet. "Gabriel!"

Her clit throbbed and pulsed. She turned her head to see him watching her with dark eyes. She wiggled her ass at him, hoping to entice. "Gabriel, come on, baby. Don't you want to come inside me, sail us both into ecstasy?"

"Tell me again that you love me," he rasped. "Let me hear the words once more."

"Gabriel, I *do* love you. I love you so much I can't stand it sometimes," she wailed. "I love you so much it scares me to death. I love you so much, I'll never leave you."

"That's what I wanted to hear, baby." He knelt and inserted two fingers into her pussy once more from behind. He didn't thrust, but let his fingers stretch and fill her. She spread her legs to give him room to rub her clit with his other hand.

"Oh, yes," she breathed. "Yes. That's so good, Gabriel."

He began thrusting in and out. At the same time, he took her clit between two fingers and rubbed it back and forth. "Mmm, you look so pretty with your legs spread like this, love." He groaned. "I want you so much. I can't wait until I can slide my cock into your sweet, warm body."

Her climax came hard and fast, making her cry out.

"Yes. That's it," Gabriel rasped. "Let it go. *Oui, ma cheri.*"

The muscles of her pussy clenched and released around his broad fingers. The pleasurable spasms racking her body made her vision go black and she nearly passed out from the force of her climax.

She collapsed to the floor, spent, her legs still spread. Gabriel petted her sopping pussy. "I can't believe how exciting you are when you come." His voice sounded strained with need.

She turned over and grinned at him. "Come on, Gabriel. I think it's pretty exciting when you come, too." She spread her thighs.

With a growl, he mounted her. In a smooth, hard surge, he sheathed himself inside her to the hilt.

Fate closed her eyes and enjoyed the feel of him within her, the knowledge that at this moment, they were truly one. "Ah, yes, baby," she panted as he set up a slow, smooth rhythm. His cock glided easily in and out of her, aided by the cream her body had made for him.

Her head fell back on a moan as he picked up the pace. She pushed her hips against him, matching his thrusts and wanting more. Fate came again. She cried out as the spasms shattered over her, racking her a second time. The muscles of her passage rippled around his cock, making Gabriel throw back his head and groan, but he didn't slow down. The thick, ridged length of him pistoned in and out of her, intensifying her climax.

On the heels of her second orgasm came her third, as hard and intense as the last two. His cock rubbed her G-spot deep within — in just the right place to drive her crazy. With every thrust he stroked the small bundle of nerves exactly right. Her fourth climax hit her hard. She sucked in a breath and let it out in a cry. The muscles of her inner walls milked his cock.

Gabriel called her name and she felt him shoot hard within her.

They lay, panting in the middle of the entryway, their bathrobes tangled around their bodies. "Oh, God," Fate groaned.

"Oh, God," Gabriel agreed, mumbling into her neck. He pushed himself to the side and pulled her close.

"I love you, Gabriel. For better or for worse, for richer or poorer, fear and all, for as long as we both shall live," she declared between heavy breaths.

He raised his head and raised an eyebrow. "Is that just because I can give you four consecutive orgasms on an entryway floor?"

She paused before answering. "Well, that probably helps," she answered finally.

He pulled her closer. "Minx."

She kissed him. "No, Gabriel. That's not why, although it is an amazing perk. Especially because of that whole immortal, eternity thing, which means I get multiple orgasms, like, *forever*. But, no, that's not why. I guess I loved you right from the start, I just fought it."

He kissed her nose. "And you're not fighting anymore?"

"No."

He rolled her beneath him. "Want to see if I can top four in row?"

She laughed. "Definitely."

Enjoy this excerpt from
ORDINARY CHARM
© Copyright 2004 Anya Bast

She walked back to the entryway where she'd seen a table with a phone. "It's here." The message light blinked five messages. Cole came to stand beside her. She hit play.

A sultry, breathy female voice filled the foyer. "Darling, this is Monique. Call me. I'm missing you." Pause. "Darren is out of town on business this weekend. Come see me. *Please.*"

Serena rolled her eyes. The woman sounded like she needed a fix. Maybe Cole *was* a drug dealer…of the carnal variety.

Beep

A perky cheerleaderesque voice was up next. "Hey, Cole, baby. This is Cynthia. I had a fantastic day with you last Saturday." Pause. Her voice lowered, got huskier when she spoke next. "Saturday night was even better. Wanna repeat? Call me back."

Beep

"Yeeeech." Serena turned away and walked toward the living. She couldn't take any more. It was nauseating.

"I guess I have a few women," Cole said, sounding mightily pleased with himself.

Was it any surprise? The man was stunning. Serena looked back in time to see him push a hand through his hair. The action defined his biceps perfectly and made hunger twist through her body. She looked away. "Yeah. Guess it hasn't really been a long time, like you said."

He frowned. "Guess not. Sure feels like it, though."

There were two hang-ups. Blessedly, the next message was not from a woman. Instead, it was an older sounding man. Serena wandered back to the answering machine.

"Hey, Cole, just wanted to let you know that we received *Fire of the Ancients*. We love it and only want a couple changes. You did a fantastic job on this game. You're the king of adventure games, man. We'll be getting back to you with more details, but you've done it again. This'll be a hit!"

"Well." He slanted her an unsure look. "I'm the king of adventure computer games, I guess."

"Apparently, that's not all you're the king of," Serena muttered.

He appeared to not have heard her. "So," he said to almost himself. "I design computer games. That explains all the equipment in the living room." He frowned and glanced at her. "Designing computer games is kind of geeky. Do I seem like a geek to you?"

"What?" She turned toward him. "First of all, there's nothing wrong with geeks. I happen to be one myself. Second of all—" She took him in from the top his head to his feet, every luscious well-defined muscle in-between, and tried not to swallow her tongue. "No, you don't look like one." Suddenly uncomfortable, she turned away. "Anyway, what the hell does a geek look like?" she finished, irritably.

"Let's explore the rest of the apartment." He turned and walked into the living room.

"Don't you want to call *Monique* and *Cynthia* back?" She mimicked their voices when she said their names. It was childish, but she couldn't help herself.

He turned back toward and fixed her with suddenly hooded and heated gaze. It was the calculating and measured gaze of a predator. Like shark that had just scented blood in the water, or a lion on an African plain that had spotted a wounded zebra.

Shit.

She took a step back involuntarily and bumped into the telephone table. "Are you jealous, beautiful?" he purred as he came closer.

"Uh." Oh, *that* was an intelligent response. Mentally, she smacked her forehead with her open palm.

"Because you sound jealous," he murmured. He reached her and cupped her cheek in his hand. "Maybe I should kiss you again and reassert the fact that I desperately want you in my bed, Serena. It was *you* that balked, remember?"

"I-I'm not jealous," she replied, tipping her chin up a little. "I just don't like to see women make idiots of themselves over a man." *Just like she was doing.* "I just don't...shit—"

His mouth came down on hers, completely stealing the rest of her thought. He seduced her lips to part and kissed her deep. All the while he rubbed his thumb back and forth over her cheek. He broke the kiss and set his forehead to hers. After making a little purring sound in the back of his throat, he closed his eyes and clenched his jaw. "Your skin's so soft," he murmured thickly. "I can't help but wonder if you're as soft all over."

Serena's breath caught. She used the table behind her to take some of her weight because her knees weren't doing a very good job of it.

He set his hands on either side of her, resting them on the table, and gazed into her wide eyes. "You need to leave, Serena. I mean it. You're not safe around me...for so many different reasons. I want to lead you to my bed, lay you out and take you over and over until the morning light breaks the night. I want to strip you, beautiful. I want to sink myself inside you."

A whimpering sound reached her ears and it took her a second to realize it was coming from her.

He pushed away from the table and turned. "If you don't want any of that, you should leave now. Because you're tempting me something awful."

Serena glanced at the door and back at Cole. He stood with his back to her. Suddenly, he shot a hand out toward the door and it opened.

She stared at the open door, her ticket out of here, out of this whole dangerous mess. If she left now, she'd be free of the whole Ashmodai thing, presumably.

But she couldn't seem to move.

She did want Cole. Of course, she did. She was just surprised, and more than a little wary about the fact that *he* wanted *her*. In her mind, she was still the fat girl in school all the boys ignored. It was hard for her to wrap her mind around the fact that this perfect, beautiful specimen of manhood—this man who could have any woman he wanted—found her attractive. No. Not even that. Cole professed to find her *irresistible*.

How could that be?

She wanted to find out if it was true, however, so instead of walking to the door and out of it like she *should*, she stood staring at Cole's broad shoulders, his tight ass and the back of his head. She *liked* this man as well as found him attractive. He was compelling, mysterious and more than a little dangerous. She found *him* irresistible.

But…what would happen when he got her clothes off and he discovered her overweight body naked? Would the fire in his eyes dim? Serena shuddered. That was something she *didn't* want to find out.

Something Brian had told her once came back in a rush, *You'd be so pretty if you just lost some weight.*

She glanced at the door, then back at Cole. She *should* leave. It would save them both some pain and anguish. She moved to take a step toward it.

He flicked his wrist. The door slammed shut.

Crap.

Suddenly, her mid was awhirl. What kind of bra and underwear had she put on this morning? She flushed as she remembered donning the serviceable blue briefs that sported tiny pink flowers and the boring white cotton bra. Not exactly alluring lingerie.

She just hadn't expected to be seduced today.

A wild laugh rose up in her throat, but it was choked into submission by the look on Cole's face as he turned toward her. A dark, predatory light graced his brown and green-flecked eyes. "You're mine now, beautiful," he murmured.

About Anya Bast:

Anya Bast writes erotic fantasy and paranormal romance. Primarily, she writes happily-ever-afters with lots of steamy sex. After all, how can you have a happily-ever-after WITHOUT lots of sex?

Anya welcomes mail from readers. You can write to her c/o Ellora's Cave Publishing at 1337 Commerce Drive, Suite 13, Stow OH 44224.

Why an electronic book?

We live in the Information Age—an exciting time in the history of human civilization in which technology rules supreme and continues to progress in leaps and bounds every minute of every hour of every day. For a multitude of reasons, more and more avid literary fans are opting to purchase e-books instead of paperbacks. The question to those not yet initiated to the world of electronic reading is simply: *why?*

1. *Price.* An electronic title at Ellora's Cave Publishing runs anywhere from 40-75% less than the cover price of the <u>exact same title</u> in paperback format. Why? Cold mathematics. It is less expensive to publish an e-book than it is to publish a paperback, so the savings are passed along to the consumer.

2. *Space.* Running out of room to house your paperback books? That is one worry you will never have with electronic novels. For a low one-time cost, you can purchase a handheld computer designed specifically for e-reading purposes. Many e-readers are larger than the average handheld, giving you plenty of screen room. Better yet, hundreds of titles can be stored within your new library—a single microchip. (Please note that Ellora's Cave does not endorse any specific brands. You can check our website at www.ellorascave.com for customer recommendations we make available to new consumers.)

3. *Mobility.* Because your new library now consists of only a microchip, your entire cache of books can be taken with you wherever you go.

4. *Personal preferences are accounted for.* Are the words you are currently reading too small? Too large? Too...**ANNOYING**? Paperback books cannot be modified according to personal preferences, but e-books can.

5. *Innovation.* The way you read a book is not the only advancement the Information Age has gifted the literary community with. There is also the factor of what you can read. Ellora's Cave Publishing will be introducing a new line of interactive titles that are available in e-book format only.

6. *Instant gratification.* Is it the middle of the night and all the bookstores are closed? Are you tired of waiting days—sometimes weeks—for online and offline bookstores to ship the novels you bought? Ellora's Cave Publishing sells instantaneous downloads 24 hours a day, 7 days a week, 365 days a year. Our e-book delivery system is 100% automated, meaning your order is filled as soon as you pay for it.

Those are a few of the top reasons why electronic novels are displacing paperbacks for many an avid reader. As always, Ellora's Cave Publishing welcomes your questions and comments. We invite you to email us at service@ellorascave.com or write to us directly at: 1337 Commerce Drive, Suite 13, Stow OH 44224.

Discover for yourself why readers can't get enough of the multiple award-winning publisher Ellora's Cave. Whether you prefer e-books or paperbacks, be sure to visit EC on the web at www.ellorascave.com for an erotic reading experience that will leave you breathless.

WWW.ELLORASCAVE.COM

Printed in the United States
27567LVS00004B/64-216